ALPHA'S SECOND CHANCE

JADE ALTERS

EVE

a hush fell over the courtroom as I began the closing argument. "Ladies and gentlemen of the jury, dozens of innocent citizens are dead because of this man," I paused to hold my hand in the direction of the defendant. I'd presented the evidence -- now it was up to the jurors to put this bastard away for good.

The bastard in question curled his lip at me, but I met his gaze head on. His sneer didn't faze me. I made my voice louder, detailing the heinous crimes Bull Payne had committed against our residents.

As I spoke, one of the jurors began waving her arm. She made short, frantic motions with one hand. With the other hand, she held up a small scrap of paper. The paper trembled, wobbling in the air. My eyesight was better than most, and I could just make out her words. *"I can tell what you are and so can Bull. Bull is a bear too. He's going to come after you. Go to the fire station. They can help."*

My blood froze. The inside of my mouth went dry. In a daze, I asked for permission to approach the bench. I fumbled out a lie about a very sudden, very extreme case of food poisoning, and the judge excused me. I left one of the junior prosecutors to do my job.

On autopilot, I got into my car. The suit jacket that seemed so professional during the trial had turned into a noose. I tossed my jacket in the backseat and unbuttoned the top of my blouse.

That juror had dropped two bombs on me.

First, apparently Bull Payne, Denver's biggest thug, was a shifter.

The second part was what really messed with my head. The juror, and most likely Bull, could tell that I was also a shifter.

It was a secret that I guarded, because not only was I a shifter, I was an omega.

In the shifter world, omegas were highly prized. They were always fertile, always conceived children quickly, and were generally sweet and amenable.

I didn't know about the fertile part, but I'd never been sweet or amenable -- not for one second. That didn't stop the bear clan I was born into from treating me like a possession.

If I'd stayed with them, I'd have been forced into marriage, forced to bear a child, and then I'd have zero say in any aspect of my life or the life of my child. My mate would have called all the shots.

I'd rather die than live like that. When I turned eighteen, I ran. I'd left the tiny town of Avon, Colorado behind, and moved to Denver.

A horn honked behind me. I jumped, startled, but kept both hands on the wheel. Just minutes later, I made it to the fire station in one piece. I managed to stay upright on the walk inside, despite the temptation to take my heels off and chuck them at the cinder block walls.

"May I see the chief, please," I said to a passing firefighter.

With a hand that shook as much as the juror's, I held up my deputy prosecutor's ID card.

Within seconds, the chief strolled out. I knew immediately he was a bear. Unlike me, he hadn't tried to cover who he was. I didn't wait for introductions. "A juror from the courthouse sent me. She said it was obvious —" I lowered my voice. I hadn't said the words in so long. "She said it was obvious what I am."

His eyebrows shot up. "Oh yeah. It's coming off of you in waves."

How was it possible? I'd been so careful. I had an alarm on every device. I had a reminder on every calendar. I had never missed a pill.

"She also said Bull was after me."

"Damn," he said. He took me by the arm. "Let's go to my office. You need to sit down. We'll get this figured out."

I didn't let anyone lead me around. I pulled my arm away. "I'm fine." I sure didn't trust a shifter to help me. There was always the risk that he'd alert my clan, and they'd come after me. Clans didn't let omegas go without a fight.

He didn't comment on my pulling away from him. "I'll do whatever I can to help."

"I appreciate that," I said as I tried to get a grip on my emotions. I might not trust shifters, and I never minced words, but if I was going to survive this, I'd like to still have a job in this town. I didn't need to burn bridges with a potential ally.

I sat in a chair across from his desk. I had to clasp my hands together to keep from pulling at my tailored suit pants. There were several places where they dug into my skin.

The store had claimed they were custom made for 'women with curves,' but they still looked liked they'd be better suited for someone with a ruler-straight figure. Maybe if I'd only done more yoga like my best friend had suggested,

I'd have flattened out those pesky curves. *Yeah right. And you could have given up those steaks you like so much while you were at it.*

I had bigger problems than my awkward clothing. I had to figure out a plan. I needed to get back to my house and find out why my scent blockers, and possibly my suppressants, had failed, then I needed to get back to work. The biggest trial of my career was happening, and I was screwing around in a fire station.

I took a long, steadying breath. If the chief was going to help me, he needed information, and at this point, he was my best option. I'd have to be frank with him. "I'm Eve Johnson. I'm a deputy prosecutor, and I was in the middle of a criminal trial, for Bull Payne."

He nodded. "We've been following the news. We're all hoping he gets life."

"A life in prison is more than Bull deserves," I said. Then I hesitated.

Why is it so hard to just say the facts?

I confronted hardened criminals on a daily basis. I spoke to news reporters in front of TV crews at least once a week, and I often had to deliver uncomfortable news to victims. Yet speaking the truth of who I was really sucked.

I sat up straight and pressed my palms over my stupid, constrictive dress pants. "You can obviously tell that I'm a bear, and that I'm an omega, although I do not acknowledge either. I wear heavy scent blockers to keep shifters from being able to find me, and I take suppressants to ward off any hormonal fluctuations." I refused to say the word *heat* out loud. At least not yet. "The juror said she could tell I was a shifter."

"I've got a few friends in high places." He eyed me. "I'll make a few calls. You're free to go, obviously, but I'd feel better if you hang out here until Bull's been transported back to the jail. After I talk to a few colleagues, we can come up with a plan."

I thanked him. I had a few phone calls of my own to make. Priority number one was finding out why my suppressants had failed. I'd heard a few horror stories, here and there. If my suppressants weren't working at all, then I would be going into heat within a week or two, whether I wanted to say it out loud or not. That was a nightmare I would not allow to happen.

Priority two was keeping an eye on this fire chief. He was a shifter, and that meant I couldn't let my guard down. He might seem nice, but if he contacted my family, I'd have to run again.

OWEN

*D*amn it all to hell. This was supposed to be an easy job. My commanding officer had promised I'd just hang around the horse race track in Denver and make sure nothing got out of hand.

My elite military unit within the army was called MASK, which stood for Military Alliance of Shifters, with a K added on for fun. Apparently because one of the founders thought the word *mask*, when referring to a shifter, was too good of a pun to skip. I'd roll my eyes, but it was a damned good group of soldiers, one I now considered family.

Thanks to MASK, we'd just finished six months working undercover in Vegas, tracking down illegal arms sales. I'd been a pretend arms dealer, and the scum I'd had to put up with wasn't fit to be called human.

Today I should've been escorting drunks to a taxi, but instead I was listening to a few morons plan to rob the place -- while I stood five feet away. Was it too much to ask for a break? I was beyond ready to get back home to Avon and enjoy my peaceful cabin in the mountains.

I wasn't sure what was dumber, these crooks thinking

they could get away with a thrown-together robbery, or planning it within earshot of me. Sure they wouldn't expect a normal human to be able to hear, but still. Race tracks were well-guarded.

Once they were on the move, I followed them. I didn't need backup, not for this.

Or so I'd thought. Too late, I caught the flash of metal as one of them pulled a pistol from the back of his pants. Before I could get to him, he grabbed a random woman and pushed the barrel of the gun into her throat.

I was too slow. He'd taken a hostage.

They were more skilled than I'd thought. The man's free hand was over her mouth, and she hadn't had time to scream. No one around us had a clue.

I had to get over myself. I'd assumed they wouldn't have weapons inside the track. Which was a rookie mistake, considering I'd just spent months watching how well-connected weapons dealers could be. I wouldn't allow my miscalculation to endanger this woman's life.

I pulled a race track ticket out of my pocket and ambled along, pretending to study the stats as I shuffled next to the hostage.

Using just a little of my shifter speed, I whipped my arm around and grabbed the gun. I pointed it at the robber's head.

"Ma'am," I said to the woman. I didn't take my eyes off the suspects. "Just follow me."

"Shouldn't I get a security guard?" she asked. Her voice was whisper-quiet.

I yanked the suspect's sleeve up. Sure enough, there was a bull tattooed on his arm. Anyone could be in on this. "No, you follow me."

As I was hauling him to the exit, my phone rang. It was

the fire chief. The only reason I answered was because he's an extended part of my clan. Anyone else could wait.

As soon as I picked up, he started talking. "I need you at the fire station now. Takes precedence over what you're doing. Orders from MASK, from the higher ups."

"I need someone here. I've got two perps and a woman who was a hostage."

"Someone's almost there."

"Got it. See you in a few." My backup arrived within minutes. We got the suspects cuffed and I took a second to speak to the poor woman who'd probably thought she was going to die, before hopping in my SUV.

It looked like I wasn't getting that promised break after all.

At the fire station, the chief met me outside. His eyes were hard. "We've got a situation. It's about Bull Payne; his trial's today."

"I'm aware. Those creeps I found trying to rob the race track are loyal to him. I just got off the phone with the guys who took over; they said they're refusing any leniency in exchange for information."

"Goes beyond that. There's a female here. The lead prosecutor. She was in the middle of her final speech to the jury, and one of them says she can smell her because she's a shifter. Says Bull's a shifter too, and he's after her."

"Suppressants," I said.

"And scent blockers. She's been using them for years. And so has Bull."

"What the hell. How did we not know that?" Even with blockers, someone, somewhere, should have known Bull was a shifter. I rubbed my face. Sometimes these things seemed harder than physical battle. We'd all been after Bull for years, and we'd had no intel about this.

"Really good chemicals," the chief said. "He's got the money."

I pressed my fingers into my temples. As a shifter I relied on my senses. The blockers created an absence, one that meant my senses were useless. I didn't know any shifters who would touch them, although I was aware there was a thriving market of shifters who did. But from what I'd heard, a shifter usually used them only for a short period of time. Bull would have been using them for decades.

There was nothing that would ever make me take a suppressant. I would never hide who I was.

If we'd known what Bull was, he never would have stood trial in a dinky state courtroom. MASK would have taken over and we'd have gotten him into a federal court.

He'd kept this charade going for a decade. Had the two idiots today at the race track been shifters?

Not likely, because they hadn't reacted to me at all.

I needed a hot shower and a steak. But first, I had work to do. "I'll interview the prosecutor. Get her to a safe house."

The chief grabbed my arm. "Owen. One more thing."

"What is it?"

"Watch yourself. She's an omega."

An omega. The word was painful to say. My first — and only — real love had been an omega.

It had taken years, but I'd gotten over her. Eventually.

Protecting everyone, human and shifter alike was my job. But an omega in danger? That was a mission I would defend with my life.

EVE

Alone in the chief's office, I made several calls to the places where I bought my suppressants. Because shifters weren't known to humans, we bought them in an underground network of shifters made up of doctors, scientists, and pharmacists.

"What do you mean, they lose their effectiveness after five years?" I said to one of the pharmacists I'd been visiting for years.

"It's common for omegas," she said, her voice crackling over the phone. "Shifters have powerful immune systems. Our hormones overpower the synthetic ones. Someone should have explained this to you."

Maybe they had explained years ago, when I was so desperate to be human. To blend in.

How had I never asked if it was a permanent solution? It was an unforgivable oversight. The blockers and suppressants becoming ineffective was a reasonable enough conclusion. I'd grown complacent, taking them for years, never anticipating the day they might not work. Had I been willfully ignorant? That wasn't like me, not at all.

Reeling, I leaned back and closed my eyes for a few seconds. The stress had my blood pressure shooting sky high. I grabbed my phone and opened up a text message. I needed to check in with my team and find out the status of the case.

As I texted, an odd feeling came over me. A wave of dizziness made my head spin. When I took the suppressants, they lived up to their name and suppressed most of the extrasensory skills I had as a shifter.

Gradually, those skills were coming back to me.

There was another bear nearby, besides the chief.

I stood, tugging at the blouse, willing it to lie flat against my generous chest. I went to the window and lifted the blinds.

Outside, the chief greeted someone. A man. A very tall, broad man with a powerful, decisive stride.

I'd seen that walk before. Many years ago.

My heart, already working overtime, sped up. The man in the parking lot was no human. It was Owen Brady. My almost-mate. And a bear shifter from my clan.

You can't let him see you.

My throat constricted. Had this been a ruse to get me back to the clan? It seemed too convoluted for that. If they'd known where I was, they could have simply grabbed me.

The reason was irrelevant. I'd worked too hard to let him take me now.

I'd thought the dual shock of finding out Bull was a shifter, while discovering my own precious chemicals no longer worked, couldn't be topped. How wrong I'd been.

I pulled my prosecutor's ID badge from my purse again and clipped it on. I grabbed a clipboard and pen from the desk and left the chief's office. I pushed my shoulders back. Any firefighters on duty would recognize the ID.

As first responders, firefighters were occasionally asked

to participate in investigations, so I'd have to hope I looked like I was on official business.

I met no one in the hallway. I ducked into the women's locker room. I shed my clothes and wadded them into a ball. I jumped into a shower, letting the hot water run over me. I soaked my hair and I dumped every shampoo I could find over myself. With quick motions, I scrubbed my entire body.

I wrapped my long hair up in a towel. Still dripping, I dug for a spare uniform. Damn it. The only two women on the force were much much smaller than I was. Maybe I should go into firefighting as a second career. I could at least sling a small adult over my shoulder. I'd be shocked if these tiny size two's could lift a cat.

Across the hallway, I found the men's extra uniforms and pulled on a pair of black pants and one of the button down shirts they wore. I spotted a can of men's deodorant and sprayed myself down with that too.

I took my ID and my purse, but left my clothes behind. They'd smell too much like an omega.

I went out the back door. I slipped into my car. As I left the parking lot, I spotted Owen walking inside the building.

I drove.

OWEN

The chief's mouth pulled tight. "She's gone."

"What do you mean, she's gone? She left Bull's trial to what? Run away?" I knew from personal experience what it was like for an omega to run away and never be heard from again.

How could he have lost a fully grown omega? I took a step closer to the chief. "Didn't you have anyone watching her?"

He held up his hand. "You need to settle down. She was always free to go." he said. "I had my men watching the perimeter. No one could have gotten inside that wasn't authorized."

I took a step back. I couldn't let my personal feelings interfere with the job. "I know you don't like hearing this, but you could have someone on the inside, spilling secrets for cash. Or because they're threatened." The Chief had never liked any implication that his men were less than perfect, human or shifter. Today, he needed a healthy dose of realism.

He didn't answer me. He turned his back to me and strode through the hallway, to the women's locker room.

"Look," he said. He pointed at a pile of women's clothes. I picked them up. It was part of a woman's black suit, with a white blouse, black pants, and black heels, appropriate for court.

The smell of honey mixed with spruce was familiar, stirring long-ago memories. I shoved the thought away. The less I lived in the past, the better. I yanked a shower curtain aside. I touched the still-dripping shower faucet. "The shower stall is still humid. She was just in here." I'd have to hope that she'd gotten spooked and taken off. If Bull's men had an omega…

"You'll find her," the chief said.

Damn right I would. We'd been after Bull and his gang for years. I wasn't going to let him hurt anyone else. I picked up her clothes and inhaled, grateful the chief was a shifter and would understand why I was sniffing a crumpled suit. "Got any pictures?" I asked. The scent of the clothes was fucking with my head. I'd only ever smelled that particular blend of honey and spruce on one shifter, and I hadn't laid eyes on her in ten years.

In the chief's office, he pulled out a file. "Yeah, we have plenty of pictures. She's got a headshot on the district attorney's website." He dropped a file in front of me. "This has her address, phone number, all of that. Her boss is in court with Bull right now, but he'll be a good resource when they're done."

I opened and picked up the papers and froze.

The woman staring up at me from the professional website photo was Eve Johnson.

Eve, who had been the love of my life, my friend, and my future mate.

I took a step back. I gripped the arm of the chair. She was not only alive, she was thriving. She was second in line to the district attorney, and she was working a high-profile case. All this time, she'd been in Denver, just hours from me.

"You okay?" The chief frowned at me.

"Fine." I swallowed hard. If I let him know she'd been my promised mate, they'd pull me off the case. "She left in her own car, right? I'm going to have the state police run a search for her tags. I'll be in touch."

I went straight to the police station. I'd served with one of the guys overseas.He'd let me use his patrol car, no questions asked. I put in a call to the state police, and within ten minutes I had a location on Eve. I hit the road immediately. She was headed west on I-70.

Any first-year yahoo right out of training could track a license plate. This wasn't the kind of work I'd usually be doing, but I wouldn't stop, not even if they did take me off the case. I had to deliberately loosen my grip on the steering wheel. Thanks to the extra strength from being a shifter, if I held on any harder, I'd rip the wheel right out of the patrol car.

I wouldn't trust anyone else with Eve, even though I knew I'd be dealing with the fallout for a long time. I had spent years getting her out of my head. And with one glossy photo, all the emotions I'd worked hard to put aside came rushing back. I couldn't stop thinking about her, and I found myself missing her presence in my life again, just as I had ten years ago.

I followed her for well over an hour before her destination became clear. She was heading toward Avon. Toward home.

It wasn't her home anymore. It hadn't been for well over a decade.

Finally. Right in front of me, I spotted her car. I checked the license number. Yep. That was Eve, directly in front of me on the freeway.

I hit the button to turn on the patrol car lights. It was time to catch up with Eve and have a little chat with her.

EVE

I was going well over the speed limit, so the flashing blue lights weren't a surprise. I'd just accept the ticket and move on. I could hardly explain to a human police officer why I was so desperate to get out of Denver.

I spotted a side road and put my signal on, turning off the freeway onto a small two-lane road.

I parked on the side of the road near some trees, well off the pavement. I fiddled with the middle button of my shirt, where it pulled tight across my chest. This shirt was clearly made for a man, and the buttons were strained to the max. The last thing I needed was some young officer thinking I was trying to seduce him by showing my breasts.

Not that it hadn't worked for my friend Melanie.

I stared straight ahead, both hands on the wheel until the officer reached my car. In the unlikely event that this officer was a shifter, he wouldn't be able to smell even an omega over all the pungent body spray I'd doused myself with.

I turned my head as the officer approached.

No. This wasn't possible.

I sucked in air. My heart hammered. This was no police officer. Owen stood at my window. He'd been sent to find me, and he'd used a patrol car as part of his scheme.

I could press the pedal down, and go. I could try and outrun Owen. However, I wouldn't get far. He'd call in other shifters as back up. At least if it were just the two of us, I might convince him to let me go.

Owen had been less of a neanderthal than the others. He could be reasoned with.

Unless he was here on orders. Owen didn't break rules. He followed orders, because that was the way things went. He thought the clan was best, for anyone and everyone.

I rolled down my window. "I will not go back to the clan. I'd rather die fighting you," I said. He was even more gorgeous than he'd been ten years ago. He'd lost the look of youth, and looked like a fully-grown shifter male.

"You haven't lost your flair for the dramatic," he said.

"Who's the one that needed a police car to chase me down?" I quirked an eyebrow at him. "Guess you needed the humans to help after all, huh?"

"I have no issues with humans. I protect and serve them just as I do shifters."

"Right." This wasn't going anywhere. Driving away it was. I pressed the gas. The car lurched forward, tires spinning in the loose gravel on the side of the road. The car bumped as I hit a few scrubby bushes.

Owen roared, and raced after me. The side of the car thunked, and there he was, grabbing onto the car with both hands.

I took my foot off the gas. "What are you, a dog? You're going to get killed chasing a car." Heart pounding, I shoved the car into park. I was terrified, and pissed off, but I didn't want Owen to die.

I scrambled into the passenger seat and crawled out the

door. I ran over scrubby brush and sandy dirt. There wasn't a lot of cover out there. I twisted my head -- he was close now.

I should've run more. When Melanie begged me to run that half-marathon, I should have done it, instead of laughing at her. My human body was not happy.

My body longed to shift. In my bear form, running came easily. It had been ten years since I'd shifted. I missed it so much.

His hand closed around my arm.

I whirled around. "Fuck you." I was pissed off that he wasn't even panting.

"I am trying to help you," he said.

Sure. Not freaking likely. "No bear has ever done one thing that would help me. Let go of me."

He didn't let go. Instead, he took both of my wrists and held on. "I am not here on clan business. I'm here to save your life."

I jerked my arms, but I couldn't get away. "I'm doing just fine on my own."

His jaw tightened. "Yeah. You were doing so fine that you were standing three feet away from Bull this morning while he scented you. Just fine."

"That was an oversight. I underestimated him. What's your excuse?"

"I don't have one. All of us have underestimated him. I won't make that mistake again. I'm not letting you go. You'll die out here."

"I can live with that."

"Well I can't."

I didn't want to die, far from it, but I refused to live a half life, confined and controlled. "I don't trust you." I also didn't want his hands on me. Later, I was going to make him pay for this. The longer he held on, the more confused my body was getting. Warmth crawled up my arms, and into my chest.

My stomach fluttered. My mind objected, but my body remembered Owen's touch as welcome, and not a threat.

"I give you my word. Whatever you're worried about, I won't do it."

I nodded my head toward my wrists, still held in his grip. "That means nothing to me," I spat at him.

His word had meant everything to me, at one time. Until I learned that he wanted what was best for the clan, and not for me.

OWEN

Stung, I let go of her wrists. My word meant nothing to her? My word, and my vows to protect, was what I valued the most. "You don't mean that."

She crossed her arms and fixed me with a withering glare. I was glad I wasn't being cross-examined by her. "Now who's dramatic?" she asked with a lilt to her voice.

"This isn't like you. Please be reasonable." I couldn't let her get away. Bull's men would end up killing her when she didn't act like a perfect omega.

"This is very much like me. The girl you knew wasn't really me; it was a sad version of who I could have been. I learned to be human. I learned to survive. And I learned to have a life of my own. One that I'm in charge of."

She should be terrified of Bull, but it's me she's scared of. I had loved her. I had thought we'd spend our lives together. Even now, I couldn't get enough of staring at her creamy skin and her full pink lips. "Why do you hate me?"

"I don't hate you. This has very little to do with you," she said.

It was hard to keep looking directly at her face. She was

even prettier than she'd been at eighteen, and I wanted her. My stomach churned. I wanted her to want me back, which meant I was setting myself up for another harsh rejection. "I have no idea what you mean."

"Our clan. Our kind. They want me to be locked away, good for one thing only," she said. Her green eyes shone in the light. "They wanted me owned, like a possession," she continued. Her voice shook as she spoke.

I hated seeing her in pain, but I didn't appreciate that she thought I wanted her treated so badly. "You were going to marry me. I didn't treat you like that."

"Why are you so dense?" Her voice rose. "You were part of the system. I tried to talk to you about it. I tried to make you understand."

Why had she rewritten our past to make me a villain? "You never said a word."

"I asked you to leave with me. I told you I'd found us a place in Canada, where we could go and be free." She looked away. "You laughed. You said no."

She was holding one conversation against me. At eighteen, I hadn't understood what she meant. Had I understood, would I have acted? Would I have left with her? I wasn't sure. "I didn't think you were serious."

"No one ever thinks an omega is serious."

My bear grumbled. I stared at her. I'd tried to give her everything an omega could want. I'd have done anything for her, and she'd thrown it away. It didn't matter. Those days were long gone. "We need to get moving. We're going to get in the patrol car, drive to a motel, and check in." I held out my hand. "Give me your cell phone."

"It's in my car."

"Good. We'll leave it there. If one of his men find your abandoned car, and phone, maybe we'll hold them off for a little bit."

EVE

The first motel we found was what you'd expect along a deserted highway in rural Colorado. Because things were going so well for me, the lady announced they only had one room, with one bed. Then she winked at us.

"Disgusting," I muttered. "Now we know why there aren't any rooms."

Sure enough. There was one bed. Lumpy, with a dingy orange bedspread. "We're lucky shifters don't get hepatitis. Or worse," I said.

Owen kicked the bed frame. "We aren't immune to bed bugs"

I shuddered.

"I'll take the floor," he said.

"No. It's fine. We both need to be rested." I raised my eyebrows. "I'll try not to paw at you." As angry as I was, it wasn't smart for me to keep picking at Owen. It was best if I acted as though we had no history.

Owen groaned. "Your jokes are still bad." He said something under his breath. It sounded like, "There was a time you wanted to paw at me."

I wasn't going to touch that one. I had loved Owen. I had found him gorgeous, sexy, and smart. I'd dated a few humans here and there, but none did anything for me. After being engaged to a shifter bear, whether it was my choice or not, human males just didn't measure up.

I snuck a look at Owen. As many males did, he had improved with age. Without the veil of anger, I could see him clearly now.

However, this was no time to get lost in ruminations. I sniffed my shirt. "Ugh. I smell like a frat boy who overdosed on body wash. I'm going to shower."

"Thank you. I was contemplating finding a bag to put over my head."

"I didn't exactly have a lot of options. It was that or spray on some fire extinguisher foam." I wandered into the cube-sized bathroom and shoved the shower curtain aside. "I'm going to have to use something else."

"Now that Bull knows you're a shifter, you could just let it go."

"Right. And invite every shifter within a fifty mile radius here. Not to mention the clan coming after me."

"I told you, I won't let that happen."

"How exactly would you prevent it?"

"I'm the Alpha now."

"You can't tell me the elders don't still hold a lot of power," I said. They'd never let go of that much control.

"They think they do. But they'll listen to me."

They might do as Owen commanded. But that didn't mean the system was any different, not in ways that mattered to an omega. "You have no idea what it's like."

"So tell me."

"I was born an omega," I said, fighting to keep my voice

steady. If I could present evidence to a jury, then I could keep from screaming at Owen. "I had no control over that. I wanted choices. I had none."

He frowned at me. "I would have let you do whatever you wanted."

I dropped into the ratty arm chair shoved in the corner. It was probably covered in lice, but I was too tired to care. "Do you even hear yourself? You'd *let* me? You're part of the problem."

"And humans are so much better?"

"Yes. They aren't perfect. And they have their own screwed up history. But now, things are a whole hell of a lot fairer for women than they are for shifter omegas."

He said nothing.

I got up and went to the shower. As I suspected, a fine layer of black mold covered every surface. It was preferable to looking at Owen's bewildered face. It was hard to believe, but he really didn't get it. I tried not to breathe in. I might have shifter immunity, but even a bear didn't want to inhale germs like these.

All these years, and he hadn't truly understood why I left. I knew he was smart, but all those times I'd tried to talk to him about how I felt, he apparently hadn't listened.

Oh well. It was better to know that upfront, than to get lost in a tangle of what-might-have-been.

Getting the stench of the body wash off was nice. This time I used the generic shampoo. It had a slightly industrial smell, like the soap at a sports arena or a concert hall. When I got out of the shower, I wrapped myself in a threadbare towel that barely covered my body.

"I don't have any clothes." I wrinkled my nose."The smell of body spray is baked into the firefighter uniform."

"I have your suit. From the courtroom but it smells like omega."

"You have my suit? That's creepy."

"I was using it to find you, dammit."

"You were tracking me like a dog!" I laughed at the look on his face. "I could call a friend to bring me something."

"Too dangerous. I'll get you something. There's a thrift store nearby."

I couldn't wait to see what he came back with. "Owen." I put one hand on my hip, still clutching the towel with the other. "I don't wear knock-off clothes brands. I'm going to need you to find a boutique."

He turned to face me, mouth slack, eyes wide.

I burst into laughter. "Some of the lessons from our clan stuck, and practicality is one of them."

"Jeez. I thought maybe being a lawyer had gone to your head."

"I work for the state, not a private firm. I haven't bought a boutique anything. Ever." Not to mention that most Denver boutiques wouldn't have anything to fit me. They might advertise plus size, but my hips didn't agree with pencil skirts in any size.

Like most prosecutors, I bought my suits off the rack. But I'd helped Melanie shop in boutiques plenty of times. Sometimes, I held the outfits up and laughed about how little fabric they'd cover on me.

Owen left, still shaking his head. At least he wasn't petty. And he didn't hold a grudge.

He came back with a pair of sweats, leggings and jeans for pants. For a top, he had a sweatshirt, t-shirt, and a tunic.

"Wow. Not bad. Maybe I need to check out the thrift stores more often," I said. I let my arms fall down and eyeballed him. "Have you spent a lot of time with women whose clothes got ruined?

He blushed. I threw my head back and laughed again. "Seriously though, thank you."

Some men I knew, human and shifter alike, wouldn't have gone after clothes for me. Especially not after I'd yelled at them. I didn't regret it though. Owen was pig-headed and obtuse about why I hated being an omega, but otherwise he was kind, and generous. It would never have worked between us, not if he still held the same primitive attitudes, but that didn't mean we couldn't get along now.

I took the softest set of clothes into the bathroom and pulled them on. When I came back out, Owen sat on one side of the bed, the one closest to the windows and door, staring straight ahead.

I couldn't help but notice the way his shirt stretched across his biceps. I laid down on the other side of the bed.

He tinkered with the lamp, turning it on and off before lying down and facing the door. "What's wrong?" I asked.

He didn't reply.

"Look," I said. I rolled onto my side and put my hand on his arm. Under my palm, his bicep was firm. I swallowed hard. It may have been the loss of the suppressants, but I wanted to run my hands up and down his arms. And then some. I wanted to press my mouth against his. I wanted to tuck my head under his, and inhale his masculine scent.

I moved my arm until I found his hand. I wrapped my hand around his and squeezed. "I may have changed, but you haven't. I can tell you want to say something. Just spit it out."

He squeezed my hand back. "I should have listened to you more. I wish I had."

I tried to say something, but found that I couldn't. It wasn't an apology, exactly, but it was close. "Thank you. Now you know better. You can listen to others in the clan who might need their leader to stick up for them."

He nodded, but didn't let go of my hand. "I'm going to sleep. I suggest you do as well."

So much for more heartfelt conversation. My mind knew him. We grew up together. We'd spent hours making out. We'd never gone all the way, because I hadn't had my heat yet at that point, and being intimate before an omega's heat was taboo for shifters. But we'd laid down together, night after night, bodies pressed close.

He smelled like juniper and fresh air, and male shifter. He smelled like home, and the life I thought I'd have, before I realized it was a cage.

I didn't want that life, but in this moment, I wanted him. Today had been a real shitshow. Months of work, snatched from me during a closing argument. Years of hiding, blown apart the moment Owen saw me.

I scooted closer to him. I pressed my body against his, as I had so many times before. There was no way he could miss the swell of my breasts pushed against his back.

He went stiff. "I thought you wanted nothing to do with shifters."

"It's not that simple," I said. I pressed my forehead against the back of his head. I knew Owen. My bear knew Owen. That was significant, even if I didn't want to admit it until now.

He let go of my hand and turned over to face me. "You want simple?"

Now my breasts were against his chest. My nipples hardened. "Tonight, I would love simple," I said.

He took my face in his hands. Heat burned through my body, down to my core. I'd never felt this way for anyone besides Owen. His lips brushed over mine as he kissed me.

He started out with light kisses, then his mouth covered mine.

I surged against him. I pressed my thigh between his legs and we moved together, rocking against each other. His hands tangled in my hair, turning my head so he could scrape his teeth over my neck. I wanted him inside me. Now.

But first, I had a confession. "I have to tell you something."

"I'm listening," he said, voice low.

Just hearing his deep voice made me even wetter. But I couldn't get distracted. This shouldn't be so difficult to admit. I wasn't ashamed to have waited this long. It just wasn't something I shared. "I've never done this before."

"With a shifter?"

"With anyone."

Owen sucked in a quick breath. "You're a vir-"

I held a finger against his lips. "Do not say it. I feel like you have the right to know, if we're going to sleep together, but don't start treating me differently based on your old-fashioned beliefs."

Owen seized my hand and pulled it away from his mouth, but he didn't let go. "Me? Old-fashioned? Well, I never."

"If the shoe fits," I said.

He scooted closer. "Don't forget that I know all your childhood secrets," he mock whispered.

I laughed. That was true. Owen had watched me taste a mud pie, when one of our buddies said it was chocolate. He'd seen me bust my ass ice skating more times than I could count, and he'd seen me wet my pants in our shifter nursery school. "You forget." I put my hand on his chest. "I know all of yours too."

He chuckled. "Oh, right. I forgot about that." His grin faded to a slight smile. "I'm glad you told me." He brushed a stray piece of hair from my face. "Would you rather wait? Until we're somewhere nicer?"

"That's very romantic of you. But I'm a twenty-eight year old prosecutor that's possibly being chased by a mob boss." I pulled my hand from his and squeezed his shoulder. "I've decided I need to live in the moment, not wait on roses and champagne."

"I'm glad to hear that, considering I don't have any roses or champagne."

"So show me what you do have," I said. I tried to lower my voice, hoping I sounded sultry instead of sick.

He drew my hand back up to his mouth and nipped my fingers with his teeth. "I plan to," he said. Feeling bold from lust, I pushed my finger into his mouth.

"Eve," he rumbled. "If you're not careful, I'm going to lose control."

"Maybe I want you to."

"You got it," he said. Owen pushed me onto my back and kissed my cheek. He rolled over and lowered his body on top of mine, and the teasing mood evaporated.

He nipped at my earlobe, which sent a sudden spark directly between my legs. I lifted my hips to meet him. He ground against me. I didn't have any panties on, so my sweats became soaked with my arousal.

He held himself up on one elbow and tugged my t-shirt up. Once my chest was bare, he stared at my breasts. "I used to imagine this moment," he said. In those days, we'd kissed and our hands had wandered now and then, but always over our clothes.

I hadn't imagined the moment, not specifically. My fantasies had been about escaping our clan. But he was well-aware of that now. I didn't need to bring it up. "You don't have to imagine it now," I managed to say.

He closed his mouth over my left breast. I shut my eyes

and let my head roll to the side, panting. This was already better than I'd expected. When he moved to the right breast, and licked over my nipple, I grabbed the sheet in my fists to keep from screaming. "Owen."

"Eve," he said. He moved on to my stomach, kissing his way down to my waist. He tugged the ratty sweatpants off, exposing my sex to the air. He tossed my pants to the floor. He moved back up to lie next to me, taking my left knee and gently pushing it up.

More cool air between my legs. I clenched them together, needing friction. "I'm ready."

"Not yet," he said. He pushed my legs apart and lowered his hand between my legs. He teased my clit with just one finger.

I thrashed on the bed, until he held me down with one hand. "If you need to come, let it happen."

I threw my head back. I couldn't control myself. How had I gone from running from Owen, to giving him this level of trust? I was no longer in tune with my bear, the way I had once been. But my bear was obviously content to give herself over to Owen.

He pushed one finger into my body. "Feel good?"

"You know it does."

He added another finger. I tugged at his shirt. "Take your clothes off too," I pleaded. He pulled away for a second, long enough to strip. I'd seen him naked, but never in this context. A strong instinct stirred inside me. I wanted his cock.

I reached down to touch his erection. I found I liked the heavy feel of it."I want this inside me."

He groaned. "Patience. It's going to hurt if you rush it."

"I can take it."

"I know you can. It's not about taking it. It's about feeling good."

He pushed his fingers back into me, this time adding a

third. It was a snug fit, but as wet as I was, it didn't hurt. He slid his fingers in and out, and rubbed my clit with his thumb. Without much warning, my body seized up, Owen gave me the first orgasm I'd ever had with a partner. I shuddered while my body pulsed against Owen's fingers.

"Now you're ready," he said. He knelt in between my legs, gently pushing into me even though I could feel his urgency.

Twenty-four hours ago, I'd have punched someone who'd told me I'd beg for Owen's cock, but in that moment, I'd never wanted something so much in my life. "Owen, fuck me," I panted, as I spread my legs wide.

OWEN

*E*ve lay in front of me, legs spread wide, her pussy glistening. Her dark hair fanned out on the pillow. Her eyes were half closed. I wanted every part of her. I needed to be inside her.

"Do you want me to use protection?" I asked. She wouldn't get pregnant outside of a heat, and shifters didn't tend to get human diseases.

"No. I want to feel you," she said.

Oh God. I'd been hard since she walked out of the bathroom in that towel. Once she told me she was a virgin, my erection had turned to stone. Now my cock throbbed as I slid the head over her slick folds.

"Owen," she moaned. "Now."

Mine, my bear said. *Don't let her run away again.*

I wish I had as much sway with Eve as my bear thought I did.

I pressed my cock into her entrance. The rush of heat surged through my entire body. I bowed my head for a brief second. I went slowly, inch by inch. Her entrance was tight, and her body resisted me. I paused and looked at her face, watching. Her jaw clenched, but her eyes were open, and focused on me.

She shook her head. "Don't stop."

I pressed forward. The feeling of her slick heat on my cock sent a shiver down my spine. I'd been with a few human women, a few shifters, and even an omega. But nothing was like being with Eve. My body and my mind knew she was supposed to be my mate. We would have spent our entire lives together, intertwined in every way, until she'd ripped her presence away from me.

I would not let the past mar our time together now. Eve was a part of me, even if we weren't together. I could finally accept that now, as I entered her body all the way.

She squeezed her eyes closed as my hips met hers. "How are you?" I asked.

"Good," she said between breaths. "Keep going."

I shifted, pulled back, and thrust into her. She wrapped her arms tight around my shoulder and lifted her head to kiss me. I thrust again, finding a rhythm that allowed us to move together. I made it for a few minutes until the intoxication of having her, and possessing her struck me with a flood of awareness. I was going to come. I let it happen, releasing into her body.

She threw her head back and moaned. "I can feel it," she said. I pressed a hand between her legs again, circling my fingers over her folds. She bucked against me, then came again, her pussy pulsating against my cock.

I kissed her forehead. I tugged her into my arms, and I found that her muscles stayed relaxed as we lay together, both of us drifting off to sleep.

We both woke up at dawn.

I gazed at Eve where she lay on her side. Her beauty took my breath away.

Last night I'd made love to her. We hadn't fucked; with Eve, sex would never be simply fucking. My bear instinctively accepted her, and viewed her as a lover.

Now that I'd been inside her, my bear thought of her as mine. Ten years ago, before the anger settled over me, overwhelming grief had consumed me. I hadn't eaten, though hunger had clawed at me. I hadn't slept, though I'd been mindless with exhaustion. I walked through my life, bereft, only finding purpose in my work with my MASK unit.

Could I recover from losing her again?

"Don't run off," I said to Eve as soon as I saw that she was awake. I wasn't under any illusions that she wanted a relationship. As much as I'd wanted her last night, I knew our new intimacy would only bring more complications. Protecting her when we weren't sleeping together was hard enough.

"Good morning to you too," she snapped. "And don't patronize me."

I was getting really tired of her attitude. I got that her life hadn't been easy. I'd even tried to apologize. Not that it had done much good. "How exactly is trying to protect you patronizing?"

"Because it implies I can't make my own decisions."

My bear rumbled. He wanted to shift, and demonstrate to Eve that she truly was his mate. To the bear, that would solve every problem. *We will absolutely not be doing that,* I warned him. "I never said that."

"I realize that you think I'm irrational, or blowing this out of proportion. I'm sure you're tired of hearing about it. Until you can understand what it's like to have no choices, just because of the way you're born, then don't speak to me."

Why was she getting to me? I had a reputation for being a

brick wall. Nothing got to me. Less than twenty-four hours with Eve, and I was ready to bash my head into this cheap plaster wall. "I am tired of hearing about it, because you rip me apart, but you don't offer any solutions."

She shoved herself into a sitting position. She yanked the sheet up, covering her breasts. "I had a solution. Leaving!"

I grabbed my own pants and tugged them up. "Yeah. Because that solves everything."

"It did for me."

"And yet you're here now, and not back in your happy life in Denver," I said.

"Do not sneer at me, Owen Brady." She slammed her hand against the hard mattress. "You're just jealous that you're still trapped in their archaic system, and I got out."

"Enough." I was done with her bullshit. "We're leaving. Get dressed, then get in the car."

I half expected her to scream she wasn't going to listen, but as she'd said, she didn't get this far in life by not having a lot of common sense. Her ire was palpable, it blazed across the room. I wouldn't wait around for any more scathing words.

I grabbed the keys and scanned the parking lot, keeping an eye out. I looked across the treeline, then walked the perimeter of the parking lot. There were no people around. No cars. No movement.

My senses prickled. My bear's presence usually pushed at me, making me bolder. Now, he wanted me back inside. *Can't go back inside, buddy. We have to get out of here.*

I didn't expect the dart. It hit me in the neck, right in the vein.

My bear had been right to be skittish. He'd sensed this incoming threat. The poison rushed through my blood. My vision swam. My hearing dulled. A misty haze washed over me as my body struck the pavement. *Fuck.* I had to warn Eve.

I hadn't sensed another shifter nearby, so whoever did this was a human, or a shifter using more of those fucked up suppressants.

Whoever shot me knew I was a shifter -- this much tranquilizer would kill a human. A sniper shot to the head with the right bullet would kill me, so they obviously wanted me alive, not dead. I had to hope the same was true with Eve. I tried to call out to her. I pushed myself up on my hands. If I could drag myself back to the room, I could warn her.

On my elbows, I made it five feet before my body went slack. I lifted my head just as Eve shoved the door open and slammed it behind her.

"Eve," I stammered. "Get back inside." My voice cracked. I wasn't loud enough to warn her, but she spotted me on the ground.

She rushed forward, kneeling on the pavement beside me.

"Get away. Drive," I said. I tried to push her away, but my arms were useless.

"I am not going to leave you here to die." She grabbed me under the arms and started tugging. "I'm getting you back inside."

"I won't die." I managed to dig my fingers into her wrist. "Eve. Go now."

She didn't go. She kept hauling me backward, not aware of her surroundings. We made it about another five feet before the shifters showed themselves.

They crept out from the motel door next to ours. Within seconds, they were on us. One aimed a gun at my head. Another pointed a gun at Eve. "In the van... get moving," the one pointing the gun at me said.

The other one poked his finger in Eve's face. "Don't get any ideas. We dosed him with triple the amount needed. He's not going anywhere."

She hesitated. I knew she was weighing her options.

The goon pressed the gun into my skull as he spoke to her. "Omega. I said get in the van. I'm planning to leave him alive as long as you cooperate."

I could imagine Eve's eyes glaring at the one that called her omega. For once, she didn't mouth off to him. She slowly lowered me back to the ground. She squeezed my shoulder once and stood.

Two of the goons tried to pick me up. I caught a faint whiff of bear on them. So they must be shifters after all. But they were still weak-ass losers if they couldn't pick me up together. I chuckled a half-laugh when the third one had to help. They stumbled around, and finally managed to drag me into the back of a passenger van.

To my relief, Eve was in the same van. We bumped back onto the highway. I fought the tranq as long as I could, but darkness descended, and my eyes fell shut.

EVE

"Where are you taking us?" My voice was steady, but my pulse wasn't. Mostly, I was grateful they'd dumped Owen in the back with us. Seeing the gun pressed against his head had shattered my illusion that I had any control over this situation.

I wanted to scream, cry, punch everyone in that car. But I didn't want them taking my reactions out on Owen.

"It's nothing you need to worry about, omega," the bigger guy said.

I bit down on the inside of my lip. My blood pressure spiked.

Do not engage, do not engage. Owen is in the back. They could kill him. His life is worth more than your feelings.

In my career, I'd had many men try to belittle me. Some were colleagues. Some were defendants sitting in a jail cell. I'd always had options on how to respond. Today, I had very few options.

I focused on the facts. There were three shifter males in the car. Their scents were subtle, as if they'd taken a large dose of suppressants one time, but not consistently. That had likely been to evade Owen's notice. Number one, the largest, was driving. Number two, the smallest, was sitting next to me. He had a gun. And number three, in the passenger's seat, was silent. He also had a gun.

"Why is your boss interested in me?" I had to ask.

The driver chimed in with an answer. "He doesn't like an omega rising above her station, never mind trying to put him in the slammer."

Above my station? Were we in 1820 and I didn't notice?

"Surely he wasn't angry that I was doing my job."

"Only a little. He likes omegas. They're hard to find, these days. He collects them. Wants you as part of his pretty little crew."

My blood ran cold. This was far worse than I'd anticipated. I'd imagined Bull wanted to eliminate me because of my relentless pursuit of ending organized crime in Denver. Prosecutors were targeted from time to time. But if he wanted me because I was an omega...

"Kinda big for an omega aren't you?" That comment came from the smaller one. I assumed he was jealous. I was bigger than many human men, but it was very rare for me to be larger than a shifter male. It must be giving this one a complex.

"Kinda small for a shifter aren't you?" I said back without thinking. Shit. It had just slipped out.

The smaller one growled, but the driver howled with laughter. "Jeez, dude, she got you." He turned sideways in his seat to point at the smaller shifter beside me. "Keep your paws to yourself. Boss said she needs to be alive."

The complicated feelings surrounding my size had not been left behind in the shifter world. Owen had always claimed he loved that I was taller and curvier than most omegas. Most were slight, petite, little wisps, with thin, wan faces and skinny arms and legs.

I was 5'9" and twice as wide as some of the tinier omegas. The rational part of me was glad for my size. I couldn't be pushed around easily.

But as a consequence, I'd stood out among omegas. And even among human women, whose size varied a lot more, I was on the larger side. And I liked to eat. This has not gone unnoticed by human dates, or human friends. In the shifter world, eating heartily was a necessity. We needed the fuel to keep pace with our metabolisms in a way that humans did not.

How many times had I finished off a steak dinner only to get a side eye from a date? More than I could count. I could also lift heavier weights than human men, and out-play them in sports. I could shoot a gun and throw a knife, not that I'd allowed any human man to glimpse that side of me.

Now wasn't the time to fixate on my hang ups. I needed a plan to deal with these shifters. Maybe I could overpower the smaller one, and grab his gun?

The truth was, I'd gotten lazy. I was able to defend myself against humans, but I'd let myself go concerning other shifters. I had stopped honing my senses.

However, now that I'd spent time around him again, I was tuned into Owen. And speaking of Owen, his breathing had changed. I focused on him as his breathing sped up. I didn't dare turn my head to look. I sucked in a quick breath as I heard a slight scraping sound from the back of the van.

With a roar, Owen burst from the back.

In the blink of an eye, he'd shifted into bear form.

In one powerful leap, he was next to me. His bear swiped across the throat of the goon in the back seat. Blood sprayed across the vehicle as the body hit the floor.

As a bear, Owen was so big that there wasn't any extra room left, but I was able to reach down and grab the gun from the dead shifter's hand while Owen pushed forward, biting the driver on the neck until he slumped over.

Blood poured out, coating the front seat. While Owen shoved his way behind the passenger seat, I flung myself into the space beside the driver's seat and grabbed the wheel. The driver's leg was still pressing the gas down. I shoved it off the gas pedal, and yanked on the emergency brake. The van lurched sideways and skidded to a stop.

The bigger shifter, the only one left alive, opened the door and threw himself out. Instead of shifting to run from Owen, he stayed human, clutching his gun.

Owen followed. But he was still sluggish.

I checked the pulse of the two left in the car. Both dead. Outside, thirty feet away, the shifter held a gun pointed toward Owen.

Owen could survive a single gunshot as a bear, but that was not ideal. He wasn't going to die on my watch, not if I could help it.

Owen might not be my mate, but I had loved him. And before I'd loved him, he'd been my best friend. We'd shared everything at one point. He'd pulled the first tooth I lost. I taught him how to dive into the lake near our home. And when it was time to try kissing, we'd practiced on each other. I would do anything to save him.

On the other side of Owen, the guy's arms shook. His skin was a washed-out gray. Blood flowed from the gashes on his head. The guy fired his gun at Owen, but he missed.

Here goes nothing. I peeled my shirt and pants off. For the first time in ten years, I shifted. The usual pain rushed over me. My bones snapped and popped.

Exhilaration reigned as joints realigned themselves. I reveled in the sun on my fur and the dirt beneath my paws. Unlike all the other times I'd shifted in my life, today I truly appreciated the power harnessed in my bear's body. Two bears, against one shifter that was in human form? Even one who held a gun? No contest.

I approached slowly. The idiot didn't realize I'd shifted.

When I was close, I opened my jaws. I let out a thundering roar. I sank my teeth into the back of his neck and pulled. Blood filled my mouth. As the life drained from him, I shook his limp body from side to side. Owen jumped on him from the front, and within seconds, it was over.

Owen butted his head against mine. And to my surprise, I let him do it for a few minutes until I itched to speak to him. I shifted back to human form, panting from the exertion.

I wiped the back of my hand over my mouth. I'd just killed someone.A fellow shifter. I'd always heard humans say that having to kill someone, even in self defense, was traumatic. Something that stayed with them forever. Maybe it was the adrenaline, but I didn't feel bad at all. I didn't like that I'd taken a life, but Bull's shifters had forced my hand. I felt capable, and strong for having been able to handle them.

Maybe it was because I was a shifter. Maybe we viewed it differently. Traditionally, our bad guys didn't go to jail. They were exiled, or they were killed. And exile for Bull or his men? That would just be sending the problem to another clan. Honestly, I'd done the world a favor by getting rid of him.

Or maybe I just had a ruthless streak. I'd have to ask Owen later how he and his team viewed having killed a fellow shifter.

But for now, Owen had shifted back as well. He stood there, naked. I couldn't get enough. I stared openly at his body, at his ripped muscles and gorgeous skin. Growing up, seeing others naked had been a part of life as a shifter. I had forgotten what it was like.

I let my gaze travel over his body, his defined chest, his

broad shoulders, his firm, flat stomach. A flush came over me; I could feel my neck and cheeks get warmer.

He pulled me toward him. "I hate that you had to fight. I shouldn't have ever let them get close enough to you to take you. But that was fucking hot." Just like he had last night, he put his hands on my face. He leaned in and kissed me on the lips.

"There's blood in my mouth," I said.

He dropped his mouth to my jaw, where he kissed down to my neck. "You've been with the humans too long if you think that's a turn off for me."

"I'm glad that you think that was hot, but we are naked, covered in blood, and standing in a field near a highway." I cocked my head. "Sounds like the start of a horror movie."

"My kind of movie," he said. Like last night, I melted against him. I let my head fall back as I moaned. He moved his lips down, from my neck to my chest, where he licked a long stripe across my collarbone.

"What would the title be?" I asked haltingly. I could barely get the words out as his tongue moved down and danced across my breasts.

"*The Bear Gets What He Wants* sounds like the perfect title."

Owen thought he was clever. Two could play at that game. "I was thinking more along the lines of, *The Alpha Has to Work For It.*"

Even as I laughed with him, the space between my legs grew wet as he stroked and kissed my swollen breasts. My knees trembled. I wanted him inside me again.

"I want you," he said.

Astounded at my own brazen thoughts, I agreed with him. "I want you too," I whispered, which was a massive understatement.

I put my hand on his face. His dark eyes, usually piercingly sharp, were a little dim. I smoothed my hand over his cheek. If he wasn't back to one hundred percent, we didn't need to be fooling around. And it was probably prudent that we watch out for more of Bull's men, instead of hanging all over each other. "I'm grateful you are, but how are you even awake?"

"My MASK unit spent about a month ingesting tranquilizers. A little bit at a time."

I looked at his eyes, trying to see if his pupils looked any different. "I thought that was a myth."

"Nope. It works like any drug or alcohol. I'm not immune, obviously, but I have a tolerance."

On impulse, I leaned in and wrapped my arms around him. "You are full of surprises."

His arms came up to grip me in a full-bodied hug. "This must have been Bull's B team if they didn't anticipate something like that." I felt him kiss the top of my head. "They didn't even cuff me."

"Noobs," I said, looking up at him. "That's what my boss's kids say."

We laughed together.

He pulled back a little. "It's all I can do to keep my hands off of you. And I would love to have you outside, but not until we've dealt with the rest of Bull's lackeys. They could be surrounding us right now and I'd miss it."

"Not into exhibitionism?"

"Not with people trying to kill you." He looked up at the sky, then turned, looking over the road and the woods behind us. "Let's get going. We either need to shift, and travel as bears, or we need to take this van back to the hotel and get the patrol car. This van could have a tracker on it."

"How did they find us to begin with?" I asked.

"Bull has infiltrated everywhere. Now that I know he's a bear, it makes more sense. He's able to reveal himself to shifters, and gain absolute loyalty. It's possible he's had a tracker on your car too. "

"Ugh. Makes me want to push the car into the Royal Gorge." I shivered. This wasn't my first encounter with a smart criminal, but it was the first where I'd been so thoroughly snowed. At least I wasn't the only one. "What's your recommendation? Shift or drive?" I asked Owen.

When I saw the smug way his lips turned up at the corners, I whacked him on the arm. "Don't say a word. Yes, I am able to recognize your expertise." I coughed. "Every now and then."

He couldn't stop the grin from fully spreading across his face. "In that case, we need to shift. That's the fastest way to throw them off." He pulled up a map on his phone. "Let me show you where we're headed."

He pointed to a tiny spot on the map east of Avon. "My safe house cabin is in Red Cliff. It's not much of a functioning town now, so we'll stay there for now."

"You know, I'm kind of looking forward to shifting again," I said. "The first time I was so focused on escaping from Bull's men that I only partially was aware of how it felt. This time I plan to enjoy it."

"Don't get too comfortable. I need you to be aware of your surroundings."

"I know. We're not out of the woods yet." I waited a beat. "Literally."

He shook his head. "I saw that coming a mile away." He rolled his eyes. "And no, I am not going to make a joke about coming."

"Too bad."

He pressed his mouth against mine. "Raincheck once we're at my cabin?"

"Definitely," I said, letting my hand pass down his back to squeeze his firm backside before we shifted.

He grabbed my hand. "I'll be thinking about it the whole way up," he said with a rumbling growl.

I lifted my head to the sun, and I let the change flow over my body. Beside me, Owen shifted into his bear. After we changed, he rubbed his nose against my fur, then he looked to the west, asking if I was ready.

I was more than ready. I took off at a slow lope, letting him catch up to me easily.

I'd thought my earlier shift felt freeing, but this shift moved beyond that into euphoria. As I'd told Owen, when I'd been focused on escaping from Bull's men, I hadn't been able to fully experience the magic of the transformation. I loved being in my human form, but I wasn't human. I was a shifter. And I'd denied that part of myself too long.

The vivid green trees on the mountains stood out in stark contrast to the clear blue sky. As a bear, I smelled the sharp pine needles, the fresh dirt, the melting snow. In the distance, I heard the call of a hawk and the beat of a wild goat's hooves.

I took off, ready to feel the wind on my face. When I pretended to be human, I was only half of myself. When I was with Owen, I had a connection I'd never find with a human. Had I done the right thing ten years ago by leaving our clan?

Could I have found another way? Could I have done it without walking away from him completely?

OWEN

e ran for several hours as bears, farther from the city, and toward Red Cliff. My bear was pissed that I wasn't taking Eve to my real cabin in Avon. He wanted her in our home.

Give it up, show off. We aren't going to push her.

"Here it is," I said as soon as we'd shifted. I'd built the little cabin myself, about five years ago.

For the first five years after Eve left, I'd been unable to stomach building something that I'd always thought we'd live in together. Eventually I moved on, I quit obsessing over her, and I constructed the cabin, board by board. I didn't live here most of the time, but it was an effective safehouse and weekend getaway.

Avon was my favorite, but Red Cliff was a good place to hide out. It wasn't even a real town now, so we were safe from all but the most avid backpackers and hikers.

I'd traveled all over the world, but I'd never found a place that was half as beautiful as the western part of Colorado. We had high mountains, but we had trees and green grass too.

"It's beautiful," she said.

Was it lame that her approval made my heart beat a little faster? I considered offering her a tour, but instead, I was going to act on her earlier interest.

I put my hand on her arm. "You want clothes? I have plenty here."

She draped her arms over my neck and breathed against my skin. "No, I feel fine just like this."

I took her face in my hands. After ten years of not having her, I wanted every part of her. Not just sex, but talking, kissing, making out. We were already naked, so my arousal was clear. She tipped her head back and parted her lips for me.

As we kissed, I let my hand wander. I rubbed her back, then let one palm rest on her backside. She sighed, and leaned in closer, which pressed her bare chest against mine. She shifted, standing with her legs apart. I put one hand on the back of her neck. I loved the way her thick hair felt against my arm. I brought my other hand to her breasts, where I gently squeezed her nipple.

She gasped loudly, and rocked against me. The motion brought her wet sex in contact with my leg. For someone who'd been a virgin just yesterday, Eve sure did know what she was doing.

I groaned at the feel of her soaking pussy on my thigh. I grabbed her backside, pulling her tight ass towards me. My cock pressed against her stomach. Needing to concentrate on something besides my own impending orgasm, I took one hand and lowered it to her pussy. I carefully rubbed one finger over her clit. She cried out as her knees buckled, and she sagged against me.

She grabbed onto my shoulders and dropped her head on my chest. "Whew."

I guided her to the couch and sat down, intending to pull her onto my lap, but she didn't follow. "I'm going to try something," she said, and she knelt down in front of me.

"Oh god," I breathed.

I never thought I'd see the day when Eve would get on her knees for me. She took my cock in one slender hand. She leaned her head forward, and a curtain of dark hair hid my view. I scooped her hair into my hand, holding it in a side ponytail. There was no way I was going to miss seeing her mouth take me inside.

She licked all the way up, before closing her mouth over the head. She sucked, and hummed and used her hand to complement the motion of her mouth.

I pressed my hips into the couch cushion, unwilling to do anything to disrupt her. "How--" I squeezed my hand into a fist to keep from coming just from the sight of her. "How did you know what to do?"

Now that she'd confessed to being a virgin, I'd gotten attached to the idea that no other male had touched her.

She lifted her eyes to mine. "My law school classmates liked to talk. In great detail." She let her mouth curve into a sexy smirk. "I may have read a few things here and there, just in case." She licked her lips. "Good?"

"Perfect," I said. "I like it that you haven't practiced on anyone else." I tugged on her arms. "Come up here."

"Caveman," she said. She straddled me. "I like it that I can sit on your lap," she said.

"I like it too." I really liked the way her curvaceous bottom rubbed against my erection, and the way her wet lips felt against me.

"Humans," she said with a twist of her hips. "Are too small. I'd break them."

I growled. "I don't want you on a human's lap." My bear's feelings on the topic were more along the lines of, *I'll rip the head off any human or shifter that touches you.* "You're the perfect size for me."

"You always said that. Even when we were teenagers."

"It's true."

She rolled her hips over mine. I was so close to losing it. I did not want to finish early. I lifted her, wrapping her legs around my waist. "You okay with taking this further?"

"One hundred percent."

I pushed a finger inside her. She was dripping wet.

"I'm ready," she moaned. "I want you inside me now."

"You're going to kill me." I tipped my head back to take a long breath. "I am not going to rush this."

"I just went down on you for the first time. You should cater to me."

"How is that different from any other time?"

She didn't get to formulate a snarky reply because I pushed a second finger inside her pussy. At the same time, I closed my mouth over her nipple. She circled her hips until I couldn't take it anymore. "Okay, you've convinced me."

I lifted her up, and positioned her over my waiting erection. She threw her head back as she slid down, enveloping my member in the warmest heat. This time, restraint was harder.

Her breasts were the perfect height for my mouth. "You feel so good," I groaned as I hitched my hips and drove into her. We didn't last long this time. She came with my mouth on her nipple, and my hand between her legs. I followed her immediately after.

Sated, we slumped together. I pulled her forward until her head lay on my shoulder. I loved being able to hold her like this. I didn't say it though -- I didn't want to spook her, and have her think she'd have to run again. It would suck, royally, but I would let her go.

Soon enough, my stomach growled. "What do you want for dinner?" I asked.

"As a human, or a bear?" She lifted her head to grin at me.

Again, I didn't want to push her too hard, but I could tell

she'd really enjoyed running as a bear on the way to Red Cliff. "You want to do a little hunting?" Hunting here was ideal, because there were so few humans.

When she smiled, it went all the way up to her pink cheeks."I would love to."

"I'm going to let my team know we're here. A few of the MASK team members will be close by until this is over. I don't want you to be startled if you see one or hear one of them."

"I'd like to meet them sometime."

"Oh, no. I can't let them do that. They'd enjoy it too much."

"They'd give you a hard time?"

"They'd never stop."

"The sooner the better then!"

I caught her around the waist as we headed outside to hunt for wild game. "Let's go."

After we shifted, she caught a squirrel, and I caught a rabbit. While we shared our meals as bears, I noticed Eve's honeyed scent, mixed with spruce was growing stronger.

Abruptly, she shifted back to human and I followed suit. She clutched at her stomach. "I feel really weird."

Her cheeks, which were already rosy, turned a deep red. "How so?" I asked.

"Everything's bright. Loud."

I sniffed the air. "You smell different too."

"Well I did just run around as a bear and eat raw meat."

"Again, not a turn off for me. But no, you smell like you. Like honey and fresh spruce trees, but more so."

Even through the flush her face paled. She blinked a few times. "I am a moron. I don't know why I didn't realize."

"Realize what?" I asked. I had no clue what she meant.

Eve rubbed her hand over her mouth. "I'm going into heat."

Clearly my body had fully rid itself of the suppressants. Now I was in heat. Supposedly, within twenty-four hours, I'd become mindless with lust. And I was out here in this cabin, surrounded by Owen's military team, being hunted by a pack of criminals.

I'd never been in heat. Usually they happened sometime after an omega turned eighteen or nineteen. I'd been in Denver by then, drugging myself with as high a dose of suppressants as I could afford at the time. An omega my age usually would have suffered through twenty of them.

I bent forward and rested my head against a tree trunk. Yesterday, I'd yelled at Owen that I didn't trust him. Now, I was going to have to depend on him to protect me from other shifters during this hellscape, or else I needed to get the fuck away from him and lock myself in a concrete room.

"Eve?"

I lifted my head from the tree trunk and rubbed at the skin. I probably had a nice impression of tree bark etched into my face. "Yes?"

"I think we should get back inside."

"Yes. Let's do that."

"Before this gets more intense, tell me what you want. I can restrain myself. I have handcuffs. I can lock myself up. Or we can lock you in the bedroom, and I can guard you. I have a taser you can use on me."

It meant a lot to me that he was offering so many options, but none of them would be necessary, besides the most traditional. "I want to share my heat with you. If you're interested."

"I was not expecting you to say that," he said. His voice was rough.

"Owen, listen. I know my leaving wasn't easy for you. I think it must have sucked royally. I've only thought about it from my perspective. But when we were running, I had time to think. You were eighteen, you were doing what you were taught. And to take it further than that, I think the clan probably thought they were doing the right thing."

"They wanted to protect you."

"Yes. They saw me and all the other omegas as something precious, that needed to be protected. It wasn't right, in fact it was very fucking wrong, but it wasn't cruel, and it wasn't evil."

"You're right. It could have been better, but everyone wanted what they thought was best for omegas."

How many times was I going to have to explain this to him? If I had a magic spell, the first thing I'd do was make Owen an omega for a month. Then we'd see how he liked being bossed around. "Adult omegas need to make their own choices."

"I know that now. And I know we haven't seen eye to eye on the clan, but I'm trying. I have made some changes to the way things work."

"Like what?"

"Like there haven't been any arranged or forced marriages since you left."

"Why didn't you say so earlier?"

"I didn't get a chance."

"You're getting one now," I bit out. I pushed my hands against my eyes. "Ow."

"What's wrong"

"Even my brain hurts." I took a step forward, but my legs crumpled under me. I didn't have time to hit the ground, for Owen was there instantly, holding me up. "It feels blurry."

"I've heard that's normal," he said.

"I've always dreaded that I'd lose control. It made me resent being an omega. The other omegas would talk about it when we were teens. They thought it was cool. They kept saying stuff like, I can't wait for the day I'm overcome by passion, and I think it's going to be so awesome to be driven insane with lust." I made an exaggerated gagging motion. "It sounded awful to me."

"How does it sound now?"

"It sounds tolerable."

"Only tolerable?"

"If you consider that before today, it would have been a big *hell no* for me." I didn't want to descend into another argument, but I wanted him to know it wasn't personal. Or rather, it was personal. If Owen wasn't the one with me, then I wouldn't share my heat at all.

I was grateful we'd already slept together at this point. If I'd been facing my first time happening during a heat, I don't know that I'd have coped.

I wasn't sure how well I was going to cope now.

OWEN

For now, Eve was asleep. But as her scent became more honeyed, I knew it wouldn't be long before she woke, craving more.

Satisfying Eve during her heat? Not a hardship. At one point, it was the thing I wanted most in the world. I still wanted it, but I was apprehensive.

I'd make sure her heat was as perfect as it could be, and then we'd part ways again.

Even if a relationship had been possible -- which I was sure Eve would reject -- I wasn't ready to give up serving with my team in MASK. As long as I was physically able, I wanted to use my skills to protect both shifters and humans. Like me, Eve had busted her ass for her career. And even after this threat, I doubted she would want to give up her position at the District Attorney's Office. She'd worked hard for it, and I wouldn't ask her to give it up, not even if we were mated.

And given Eve's opinions on our clan, I doubted she'd ever want to mate.

As the Alpha, could I have a partner who wasn't my mate?

Could I have a casual girlfriend? No one in our clan had ever had such a half-assed relationship, but I'd be willing to give it a shot for Eve.

I wouldn't walk away from my MASK team, but if our clan and my family couldn't -- or wouldn't -- change enough to accept Eve on her terms, then I could walk away from my role as Alpha.

If I ditched my clan, my family would flip out. They enjoyed having me in charge.

I'd chosen the clan over Eve before, even though I hadn't fully realized it. I wouldn't do that again, if she gave me the opportunity to try again.

Did I want Eve back? Yes. However, I knew now that I'd never really had her.

The anger I'd had over her leaving me had begun to fade as she explained how trapped she had been. I'd been too young and self-absorbed to comprehend that.

I must have absorbed parts of it though, because like I'd told her, I'd worked to introduce few changes over the years to improve life for the clan. From her perspective, I could see my changes had been sadly lacking.

I knew how much I valued my autonomy. I put myself in her shoes. I imagined that someone else -- even Eve -- had the power to deny my application to MASK. Or to keep me from joining the Army at all.

My stomach burned. I'd have run too.

She'd always had not one, but two feet out the door, while I lived in ignorant bliss. It was clear to me now, a decade later, that she had tried to signal to me that she wasn't willing to accept the role of omega in our clan, but I'd ignored her messages.

Sharing her heat with her could easily backfire. But I wasn't going to let that happen -- I was going to prove myself. Trusting an Alpha during her heat was monumental.

As an Alpha, I couldn't imagine the lack of control. It was far different than just sleeping together normally.

Many unmated omegas chose to lock themselves in a room with bottled water and energy drinks. I vowed to make sure Eve didn't regret sharing her heat with me.

Eve rolled over in bed. She'd worn one of my t-shirts to bed, and the creamy skin of her chest was visible.

I went from semi-hard to rock hard in an instant. My cock throbbed. Under the thin cotton fabric, Eve's nipples hardened. I brushed my hand over her breast. Her back arched, pushing her breasts forward.

Still asleep, she moaned. She turned over suddenly, twisting the sheet as it turned with her. She kicked, throwing the covers off. She wore no underwear. Her round backside lifted and she pulled one knee to the side, exposing her wet pussy to me. The scent of honey rose, intoxicating me.

I put my mouth next to her ear. "Eve, you ready?"

Her eyes were still closed but she nodded her head. "Owen. Yes."

I pushed her knees up under her body. I ran my hands from her head down to her ankles. She arched her back even more as I caressed her skin. I trailed one finger all the way down her spine, her backside, and over her pulsing sex. She writhed against the bed, pressing her breasts into the mattress and her backside into the air. "Like this," she said. "I need it."

You need this too; don't screw it up.

I pushed two fingers into her. She rocked back against me. "Owen! Please!"

I couldn't deny her any longer. I grabbed a condom and put it on. Thankfully I'd had some stashed in the cabin. I got on my knees behind her upturned bottom, and I pushed my cock in to the hilt. Flush against her body, I bent over her. I brushed her hair from her neck, and bit the back of her neck.

She made a loud keening cry, and jerked against me. I got back upright and held onto her hips with my hands. The sight of her stretched out in front of me, on her knees, with my cock buried in her pussy with her sweet, honey scent filling my nose would be one that never left me.

I knew then, that even if Eve rejected me again, I'd never take another mate. She was it for me.

"More, Owen. More," she begged. She made little rotating motions with her hips, back and forth, pushing me to the edge. I bit down on my tongue. I wasn't going to come yet -- this was about more than just pleasing her. This was about making sure she got what she needed from her Alpha.

I wasn't hers, though. I had to remember that.

My bear wasn't happy. *You could be hers, dumbass. And she could be yours.*

Not helpful. I rolled my hips, thrusting into her, working to hit the spot omegas said felt the best.

"Yes!" she yelled. "There!"

I got one hand between her legs, where she was soaking with arousal. I rubbed small circles over her clit until she finished, her warm core tightening in waves around my cock. She collapsed, flat onto the bed, and I followed her down as I felt my own release pumping relentlessly into the condom. As much as I wanted to feel her completely, we just couldn't risk it with her being in heat.

I love you, Eve.

No. I cared about her. It wasn't love.

I had to remember that, even as I treasured the feel of her warm, pliant body against mine.

~

Forty-eight hours after she'd first noticed the symptoms, Eve stretched her arms above her head with a soft sigh. "It's almost over," she said.

"Happy to be rid of the mindless lust?" I suspected she was, because I was fucking relieved. As much as I had valued Eve choosing me to get her through her heat, and as much as I had loved getting to fuck her hour after hour until we were both spent, I was ready to watch out for Bull and his men myself, without having to rely on my team.

"I'm relieved to be able to think clearly again, but I did thoroughly enjoy this."

I'd thought she felt that way, but it was nice to hear her say it out loud. "Me too." I inhaled her scent. Our scents were now intertwined, mixed together after her heat. My bear really liked that.

"Now that I'm not incoherent, I need to check in with work. Do you have a burner phone?"

Back to the real world. "Yeah. I'll get you one." I didn't stop myself from appreciating the view as she let the sheet slide down around her waist. I could look at her bare breasts forever.

"Thanks. Luckily, I have my boss's cell memorized; I've dialed it from the office landline plenty of times."

I pulled a new phone from the safe and handed it to Eve. All of my team kept three spare phones stored at all times, as well as a packed 'go bag' and extra cash. Eve gave me one last kiss and pulled on one of my sweatshirts. While Eve stepped into the kitchen to call her boss, I stripped the sheets off the bed and picked up the pillows we'd managed to fling around the room.

Eve returned within minutes. She stood in the doorway. Her bright green eyes clouded over. Her mouth was in a flat line.

"Eve." I grabbed her shoulders. "What is it?"

"I talked to my boss," she said, with zero inflection.

What the hell had happened to make her lovely voice a monotone? "And?" I asked.

She rubbed both hands over her face a few times before speaking. "The bastards burned my house to the ground."

Fuck. Bull had moved fast -- faster than I'd expected. He obviously was still calling the shots. Had he been trying to harm Eve with the fire, or just send her a message?

"He was supposed to be in isolation at the jail. No communication other than his attorney," she said. She leaned against the doorframe and dropped her eyes to the floor.

"There are probably guards on the inside." I wanted to head down there immediately and start interrogating witnesses. And by interrogate, I meant kill. "I'll call the fire chief. See if they have any evidence."

"Thank you." She lifted her eyes back up to meet mine. They were still dull, lacking the bright green sparkle I had come to look for. "I saved up for that house. I bought it a year after I got my job." She sighed. "My boss said it's a total loss. Sounds twisted, but I want to see it. I want to see what they did to it."

"You're not going alone. I'll take you as soon as I can." I ducked my head and pulled her close until her forehead rested against mine. "We'll figure this out."

She must have really been rattled to not respond to my order that she wasn't going alone.

"I hate the thought of people picking through my charred stuff while I'm not there," she said.

"Not much we can do to stop that."

"I know. It's part of the process. I'm just wondering what else he's going to do before this is all over."

I was wondering the same thing. Creatures like Bull often escalated their warnings, with carefully plotted messages designed to create paralyzing fear on the part of the victim.

After sharing her heat, my bear insisted on being within arm's reach of Eve, and I wanted that too. But the need to get out and take action against Bull gnawed at me. My bear needed to let the world know Eve was mine, and I needed to make Bull pay for what he'd done to her.

62

EVE

Owen had not stopped pacing since he'd found out my house went up in flames. Initially, my mood had plummeted, and then my mind went blank. But as the shock faded, I was grateful that I was with Owen, instead of alone in Denver.

That was a new feeling, one I'd need to process once I had enough time.

"I'm going to check in with my team," he announced. He disappeared for a moment and came back with a rifle and a gleaming hunting knife. "You remember how to use the rifle?"

"Yes." To appease him, I took the ammunition from his hand and loaded the rifle, then unloaded it again to show him I knew what I was doing. I needed a shower, badly, but I figured I'd wait until I saw what he was up to.

"Good. I'll be back in a minute," he said.

I watched him step onto the porch as a human. He tugged his t-shirt off. Ah. He was going to shift. Before that happened, I took the time to appreciate the view.

Over the last two days, I'd had time to admire his well-carved abs, but I didn't think I'd ever tire of looking. If Owen weren't so agitated, I'd go out there and interrupt, just to run my hands over his sculpted shoulders and chest. He dropped his shorts next, revealing himself. To my surprise, my mouth watered. I had to stop myself from going out there and getting on my knees in front of him.

Do it. Let him know he's yours.

I stumbled backward and rammed my hip into the countertop.

That was the first time I'd heard from my bear in years. The sentiment wasn't spelled out in words, but the idea was clear.

I wasn't quite ready for a declaration. Rubbing my hip, I took the knife and the rifle with me into the living area.

I loaded the rifle and laid it next to me on the coffee table. Owen didn't want me logging into any of my accounts from his computer. He was afraid Bull's men would be able to find my location if hackers had accessed my accounts. Unfortunately, I agreed with him, which meant I had very little to do, now that my heat was over and we weren't actively running.

Normally I'd have relished a few days in a cabin in the mountains, with time to read and take baths, but under the circumstances, I was climbing the walls. During a few of my more lucid moments during my heat, I'd torn through the two novels he had that I hadn't read.

I thought of my own stack of hardback novels by my bed. The copy of *The Adventures of Sherlock Holmes* I'd bought in London. The first edition of *Little Women*. The cheap paperbacks I kept to read during those infrequent long baths.

All of them were gone. Turned to ash because of Bull.

Ugh. I was sick of my life being dominated by this mob boss. I dug through Owen's living area cabinets under which I found a pack of cards. Maybe I'd suggest a game of strip poker once he got back. Surely it would lift my gray mood.

As I was shuffling the cards, Owen slammed into the cabin. I had the rifle in my hands before I realized it was him.

Owen was wild-eyed. His chest heaved with every breath. I lowered the gun. I unloaded it, making my movements slow and deliberate. I stood and made my way over to him. "Owen? What is it?" I asked.

Owen ran his hand through his hair until it stood straight up. "Bull escaped."

"Escaped?" I should have considered that as a possibility. In all the scenarios I'd imagined, Bull would remain locked away in the county jail until his sentencing.

I stared straight ahead into the fireplace. We'd just wondered what Bull would do next, and that had been when we'd thought he'd be working from a jail cell. Now he was free. It was unlikely he'd head straight for us himself, but he wouldn't leave us alone, especially not after we'd killed his three men. That was an insult to him, a humiliation.

Would Owen's cabin be the next to go up in flames? With us inside?

Would Bull target our clan? I didn't want to live by my family's rules, but I sure didn't want any of them harmed by Bull. "We need to warn your clan. They're probably in danger."

The sound of cracking wood brought me out of my daze. Owen stood by the splintered side table. It lay in pieces on the floor. He shook his hand out.

I took his hand in mine. The skin was red and scraped raw, but not bleeding. "Did you break anything?" I ran my other fingertip over the bones.

"No. It's fine." He pulled his hand away. "I've warned our family. My second in command there helped get everyone into a few houses that are well-guarded."

"I should have known you'd have thought of that."

He shrugged. "Part of the job."

I knew he'd say that. "Your job as a soldier or your job as the clan's Alpha?"

"Both."

"Owen. I know you. I know you're used to busting your ass for each and every case, and now this one is personal, a lot more personal than most." I chewed on my lip. "Has the clan ever been in danger before?"

"Not since I've been the Alpha."

The threat against me and the clan had to be making Owen crazy. He wouldn't tolerate the lack of action for much longer, I could see that clearly.

"If you decide to do something, will you let me know?" In a way, it hardly seemed like a fair ask, considering our history. But I was going to ask it of him anyway.

"Do something like what?"

"If you decide to leave and go after Bull yourself."

"I'm not leaving you unprotected," he barked.

"Your team is here."

"Not good enough." He said each word slowly, over enunciating. I got the point.

Not good enough? Owen had told me he trusted his team like they were his brothers, but I recalled the lessons I learned as a young teen. A bear shifter Alpha was intensely possessive of his mate right after sharing a heat with her. Was he thinking of me as his mate, now that we'd shared a heat?

And if he was thinking of me as a mate, how did I feel about that?

OWEN

An hour after we'd found out Bull had escaped from jail, I dropped an empty duffle bag on the table in front of Eve.

She stood at the kitchen counter, making lemon chicken, continuing her quest to eat all the meat I had in the cabin. I wasn't sure how she was hungry. I had no appetite.

"I called Fort Carson Military Base," I told her. "I updated them on our situation. We can stay there, and we'll have some real backup. It's three hours away by car."

"Wait. Slow down." She laid the spatula she was holding on the bar. "I thought your team was our back up."

"They are. And they're the best trained soldiers you'll find. But there are six of them, and we're in the mountains, without any heavy equipment." I wasn't going to keep sitting here in the middle of the mountains, doing nothing, leaving Eve as a target.

"Equipment?" She frowned at me. "Like a tank? A missle? What exactly do we need?"

"I don't know. That's the problem. Most criminals are somewhat predictable. In some ways, Bull has been. But the fact that no one knew he was a shifter worries me." From my go bag, I pulled out a stack of cash and counted it. "I don't want to be caught off guard again."

She turned away from me to wash her hands at the sink. "You're doing a great job," she said.

I stared at her shapely backside as she stood at the sink. I was struck by the emotion that pooled in my stomach. It sat heavy like a rock.

Not only was she my mate, I knew I was in love with her.

I could admit it now. It wasn't the leftover feeling I'd had as a young man. It was a new love, based on the time we'd spent together. I loved her wit, her resilience and her willingness to stand up to me and anyone else in the world… I also was insanely attracted to her and never stopped wanting her with me, naked and willing.

But she didn't feel the same way.

Convince her, my bear said. If only it were that simple.

"I'm not going to be lax about this. Not with your life."

She dried her hands and put the chicken into a baking pan. "I know you won't. And I appreciate that." She put one hand on her hip as she studied me, a gesture I usually loved. I didn't love it when we were discussing how much danger she was in.

"Now tell me what would happen if we went to Fort Carson?" she asked, going back to the food as she opened the oven and slid the pan inside.

"The pros are that I could work that, to an extent, doing paperwork or deskwork. No one's going to let me take the lead investigating Bull now -- I'm too close to it. But I could do some research on other cases. If your boss approved, you could work from there as well. Even if Bull could trace us there, he can't get inside the base."

"Cons?" she asked.

I knew she'd approach this just like any other problem.

She'd want facts, she'd want to analyze. Talking with Eve was a far cry from my usual interactions with non-military. Usually if I talked to a civilian, he or she just freaked out, ran around screeching and didn't think beyond his or her own panic. Not Eve. She kept a cool head at all times. "He could already have a man inside. A shifter. Someone loyal to him."

She walked over to me and slid one arm around my waist. "How long would we stay?"

I needed her closer. I pulled her in, wrapping her in a tight hug. "Until Bull is recaptured."

She didn't push back, but sank into my embrace. "Well as we've seen, he won't necessarily stay that way," she said.

The fragrant smell of the chicken dish filled the kitchen. "We need to handle this the shifter way. He needs to be eliminated," I said.

She nodded. "I agree," she said against my chest.

"I'm surprised," I said.

"Why?"

"Because usually government lawyers are not in favor of execution."

She tipped her head back to meet my eyes. I was relieved to see her eyes were back to their usual bright gleam.

"I guess I'm more bear than I realized," she said.

My bear glowed with contentment at her statement, not caring about the context. Was it a mistake for me to hope we could have a future together? "You'd have made a good soldier."

"Thank you. I'm glad you realize that." She pointed her finger at me and tapped me on the chest with it. "That's another thing the clans don't let omegas do."

I felt unequipped to have this discussion while my mind was so preoccupied with her safety. She was right though. And I knew it. It was just taking me awhile to adjust my mindset. "They'd say it's because omegas have heats."

"That's what leave is for, or suppressants."

"That's a good point." I rested one of my hands on her lower back. Even when we weren't in bed, I wanted my hands on her.

"I'm glad you see that."

"Hey, I'm willing to listen."

She leaned up and kissed me on the nose. "Speaking of execution, I killed that shifter without hesitating."

What did she mean? That comment had come out of the blue. Was she upset about what happened?

"I remember," I said. It had been unspeakably hot. Once I'd shifted back into human form, I couldn't get the image of Eve ripping into Bull's thug. She hadn't hesitated. She'd acted, and got the job done. She really would have been a great soldier.

After the tranq had worn off and I'd been thinking clearly, I'd felt terrible that Eve had been forced to act in that way. I had avoided bringing it up because I didn't want to make her relive something so brutal. "I'm sorry you had to do that. I wish I'd been able to handle it."

She tapped my arm with her fist. "Don't even say that. You might be the Alpha, but they shot you with a triple dose."

A vice tightened around my chest. A couple days ago had been so close. Eve might be calm about it, but I wasn't. "If I'd been more aware --"

"Stop. Sure. If you'd worn full body armor, maybe. But short of that, no one could have acted differently. You saved me by leaping up into the car. They're after me, not you. You didn't do this. They did."

I nodded. Eve might be the only shifter in the world that could get me to stop arguing. The clan would say that meant she's my mate, and the only one made for me. There was no magic involved, not spells or pre-ordained soul mates. Just the fact that most Alphas only found one mate, and that was it. For life.

It was becoming clear to me that Eve was that mate for me. Now she was looking at me with her head cocked. "Are you okay?" she asked.

No way in hell was I going to let the word mate spill out of my mouth. "Yes. Keep going. I'm listening."

"I've been in the legal system for a while now, and I've worked with law enforcement officers quite a bit. They always say it's difficult to kill someone. And they really struggle with it. I know they do; I've sat with friends and listened to their stories. But I'm not upset."

That was a relief. If she had been traumatized, we didn't have a lot of options for dealing with it right now. "I'd say it's the bear part of you. We operate more on instinct. Bull's men were a threat to you, and you acted. Humans spend more time thinking and evaluating. We know that Bull poses a threat, and we want to end that threat."

I wouldn't let myself consider that she'd acted to protect me as well. She shouldn't have had to, but she had. She was tapping back into her bear, which was a good thing, if you asked me. It meant she'd be safer, in every part of her life.

She let go of me and dropped onto one of the barstools. "I don't want to go to the military base."

I braced my hands on the back of the chair, my bear still pushing me to stay close to her. "Yeah? Why not?"

"It's just going to delay whatever's going to happen."

As always, her insight was correct. "You're right."

Her forehead creased as she looked up at me. "They why did you suggest it?"

I ran my hand through her hair, letting the silky strands flow over my fingers. "Because it's the safest option for you."

"Yeah, that is not a consideration," she said. "Remember, I left at eighteen. I went to college, law school and got a job, all on my own. I appreciate your protection, but I am not someone who needs decisions made for her."

I get that. I really do. But I also can't help it. I get that you aren't my mate. But my mind still thinks of you that way, at the very least, because I am driven to protect you. I just managed to keep a lid on the flood of words that wanted to bust out of my mouth. Jeez. She didn't need to hear my inner monologue.

She let me brood in silence for a bit.

"Let me think about our options for staying here," I said. I wouldn't make her any promises I couldn't keep. I also figured that if I left to go after Bull, she'd be right behind me. "I'll let you know what I decide."

She grabbed my hand. "Come on. That chicken has another twenty minutes to go. Let's go shower." She stripped her shirt off and let it fall to the floor. "Together."

Finally feeling like smiling, I swept her up into my arms. "Now that is a good idea."

fter a morning spent contemplating my incinerated house, and the escaped prisoner that wanted us both dead, Owen and I spent a lovely afternoon first in the shower, and then in the bed.

It had become clear to me that I was falling in love with him. Not the kind of love I'd had for him as a teen, where I loved him because of proximity and shared experiences. But a true, adult love, where I respected him.

What was I going to do about it?

I had no idea. It was going to have to be a problem for another day. Making any big declarations in the middle of a crisis was definitely a bad idea.

For now, we needed something to distract ourselves until we had a plan for dealing with Bull. "You have any wood?"

"Of course," he said. "It's on the back porch. Want a fire?"

"I'm craving some meat cooked on a real open flame, not a grill."

On the back porch, Owen gathered an armful of wood and dumped it into what looked like a fire pit. "You're really embracing this bear life," he said.

That was the truth. But I also wanted a nice little distraction for the two of us. "Listen. Do you know how many hours I've sat in trendy Denver restaurants eating delicate little food that looks pretty but barely fills you up?"

He laughed. "I'm guessing a lot of hours?"

"More than you can count. My friend Melanie is a vegan. Most of our other friends are vegans. Every Friday night, we used to go the hot new restaurant, where they served the most spartan plate you can imagine with kale, chard and asparagus. Then my friends inspected every ingredient, which was usually only salt and pepper. Did you know there's meat in certain candy? They won't touch it."

Owen rifled through an outdoor cabinet and found some matches. "How the hell did you stay quiet during all that?"

"I'd sip my margarita, or my wine, or my fancy microbrew beer."

He threw some kindling on the pile of wood, and stuck the match. "Must have been a lot of margaritas."

"Luckily we don't get drunk easily."

"Or maybe that made you unlucky."

I laughed and tried to tackle him but he evaded me. He dodged me and made it back to the freezer. "Hunt for fresh meat or defrost frozen?"

"Defrosting's fine." I raised one eyebrow. "This time."

He flashed a big grin at me, and in that moment, he looked exactly like the boy he'd been at twelve, when we planned a fishing trip without permission. "I have elk, deer, duck and rabbit," he said. "What's your pleasure?"

"Deer," I said, recalling a very similar conversation when we'd been fourteen and gone camping together in a group. Nostalgia for the boy he'd been and the home I'd given up struck me hard. I decided to wade in. "I've been wanting to ask about my family." I bit my lip. "Do you ever see my parents? I mean, other than in large groups?"

"Yes. I see them frequently. At least once a month." He laid the deer meat on a plate and we headed back out to the fire pit. "They ask about you. I think they'd love to see you."

I wasn't so sure. I needed more information, but I wasn't ready to hear the details yet. We roasted the meat over the open fire, avoiding the topic of my family. Once the meat was cooked just a little, we dug in, relishing our deer steaks when a rap sounded on the front door. We both jumped. "Stay here," Owen said.

Of course I didn't stay there. I trailed Owen through the cabin to the front door, where one of his MASK Team members was standing on the front porch.

"We've got chatter that Bull is in Keystone," the shifter said, handing Owen a paper mat with a location marked map.

"What the hell?" Owen held the map up. "Did he stop to ski? Get a hot chocolate? Maybe a fucking massage?" Owen kicked the railing of his cabin, but his teammate didn't flinch. "Probably wants to blend in with the crowds there." He dropped the map. "Thank you. Check in with me in four hours, even if there's nothing new to report."

"Yes, Alpha," his teammate said.

Once he was gone, I didn't try to pretend like I hadn't listened in. "They call you Alpha?"

"Yes. It's my title, and a good call sign."

"I think I might give it a try too. Maybe a little later." I sauntered over to him and raised up on my tiptoes. I whispered, "Alpha."

"Eve." He pulled my hand to the front of his pants. "Feel what you do to me.".

"I feel it. And I like it." I gave him a quick kiss. "I need to shift and go out again. Ever since the heat, I've been craving time as a bear."

I could have seen the glint in his eyes a mountain away.

"Owen. Come on, don't be an ass. You don't have to rub it in that I am actually enjoying this a little!"

"I'm not saying a word." Owen fought the grin that pushed his lips up at the corner. "I'm glad you're wanting to do thing shifters like again. There's a creek just down the road. Let me just notify the team that we're heading out."

At the creek, I shed my clothes as soon as the fast-moving water was in sight. "Race you," I shouted to Owen right before I shifted and jumped into the stream.

After a long swim, we sat on the bank to drip dry. "I'm ready to go after Bull. Either I'm going after him, or we're both going to Fort Carson. We can't keep waiting here," Owen said.

"I agree that we can't keep waiting. But he's after me. So I am going to be involved in this."

Owen nodded, although I could tell he wanted to argue with me. "We know Bull's probably on the move. But I don't want to go to Fort Carson. I want to try to get him here," I said.

"Draw him out, you mean, before he attacks."

"Exactly," I said. "He's after me. So he'll end up here if I lure him out."

Owen placed both palms on the ground. "No fucking way are we using you as bait."

"I know it's hard, but you don't get to decide that." I willed myself to stay calm and not start shouting. "Remember, I'm here because I choose to be." The stone-faced look Owen was giving me did not encourage me to remain calm. Not one bit. I tapped him with my leg. "If you'll chill out and listen to me, I'll listen to you too."

Owen growled. "I like it better when I can just give orders."

"So does everyone else, buddy." I scooted closer to him. "My scent is still strong, isn't it? From my heat?"

"Yes. It's very noticeable."

"So let's use it. Bull was after me because I'm an omega. Let's use my scent to lure him in."

"On what planet do you think I'd agree to that?"

I scoffed at his nerve. "The one where it will work."

"I'm not comfortable with this, at all. I think we'd do better to try and lure him in with a decoy. We could trick him, using your scent. I've seen it done in the Army."

"I won't be sidelined for this." I put my hands on his shoulders and stared him directly in the eye. "You promised."

He was silent for a long time. "Okay, fine," he said after a drawn out few minutes of quiet. He held his hands up. "But we work with my team, and you let me take the lead on defending you."

"I can do that."

"Good. Now first order of business. I assume your boss is bugged, and that he's being followed," Owen said.

He wiped his hands on the towel and picked up one of the secure phones he kept. "Call him. Make it obvious where you are. Tell him you've heard that Bull is headed to Arizona. Tell him your phone is secure, and then describe this awesome little town where you're staying. Don't name it; that might be too obvious."

"While you're doing that, I'll update my team," he said as he laid the phone in my palm.

My mouth opened as my hand closed around the phone.

I threw my arms around his neck and jumped on him in a hug so strong it knocked him backwards. "Thank you." I kissed him hard on the mouth. "Thank you so much for getting this. Thank you for understanding what it means to me."

Was it possible that I'd finally have a partner who saw me as an equal?

Much to my extreme displeasure, the plans were laid out. Eve had called her boss. My entire MASK team was up to date, and our security detail was ready to roll. Now all we had to do was wait for someone to get visuals on Bull.

Behind the cabin, Eve and I were going through drills. First we'd practiced shooting with a rifle, then with a shot-gun, and then a handgun. Next we'd practiced grappling, and shifting quickly. Now we'd moved onto knife throwing.

Eve sharpened the blade she had before aiming it at the nearest tree. I didn't practice with targets for knives -- in an actual fight, no one was going to hold a piece of specially crafted Cottonwood for you to aim at.

"Last week, before all of this had happened, I got a job offer," she said. Her knife sank flawlessly into the tree.

She kept practicing, and on an outdoor table, I laid out all the firearms and ammunition I'd stocked in the cabin. In the woods nearby, my team was doing the same thing.

I had fourteen guns and twenty knives. I also had a supply of flash-bangs, smoke grenades and three drones. Two of my teammates already had drones in the air. One was searching the woods from the sky, while one was searching the roads. "Oh yeah? What kind of job?"

Eve laid the knife down on my table. "A district attorney's office in Chicago. I met one of their elected officials at a conference, and they liked an article I wrote."

Chicago? She was thinking of moving to Illinois and she hadn't mentioned it at any time in the last few days? How the fuck was that possible? Now she chose to bring it up while we were testing our weapons, knowing we were about to be attacked again? My back stiffened. The blood in my veins sped up, rushing through my body, causing my heart to pound.

I didn't think I'd ever understand Eve. "Not many bears in Chicago. Real or shifter," I said.

"No. It's not really a place where many shifters of any type gather."

"Maybe those who don't want to be shifters," I grumbled.

"Are you implying I didn't want to be a shifter?" She asked, as an edge crept into her voice..

Wasn't that exactly what she'd said? I was under the impression she'd rather have been human. "Now is not the time to get into this."

"When exactly is the time? After we're dead?" she said.

"What does that even mean?"

"We could die doing this." Eve snatched a knife off the table and flung it, slamming into the tree so hard bark flew off

"I'm well aware. That's why I find it odd that you bring up the fact that you want to move to a place with no shifters!" I tried to stop my voice from rising, but it got louder without my consent.

"I didn't say that!" Eve yelled.

I rubbed my hand over my mouth. I couldn't stop a harsh exhale. "That is exactly what you said!"

"I was telling you about an opportunity I got. Then I was going to ask how you felt about me moving, you idiot!"

I had no idea what to say to that. I stood in silence for a few moments while Eve picked up a gun and fired several rounds into one of the shifter-shaped targets I did keep for shooting practice. She was still a good shot. She always had been, even when we were kids.

Had Eve been testing me? Trying to see how I'd react? Was I supposed to ask her not to go? No. She wouldn't set me up. She'd just say something. She'd tell me what she wanted, or she'd ask me what I wanted to give.

Every part of me wanted to slink into the house and turn on the television, and numb myself to the agony of trying to deal with an omega you loved, but couldn't have.

I wouldn't though. I was the Alpha. I dealt with problems head-on, or so they told me. I wasn't going to wimp out and hide from this, no matter how much I wanted to.

I took a few steadying breaths, and walked around the perimeter of the cabin. No one in this world pissed me off like Eve did. And yet, no one else made me feel as alive.

It was time for me to grow up and tell her how I felt. I could stand around and wait for a clear signal, or I could take action. The worst thing she could do was tell me off, or never speak to me again. I'd already survived that heartbreak once. Thousands of people and shifters alike suffered far worse things on a daily basis. I could do this.

When I got back from my walk, Eve sat cross-legged on the ground, sharpening each knife with precision. She fixed me with a strident glare but didn't comment.

I sat down on the ground next to her. "I'll get right to it. I am in love with you. I want you as my mate. Not because you're the one that got away, but because I've fallen in love with the adult you. The one that's brave and fiery, and who doesn't hesitate to get in my face."

I cleared my throat. "When you said you wanted to move, I didn't react well."

Eve's mouth dropped open.

"Now that we've cleared that up, we can get back to planning our strategy."

"I won't leave again," she said.

I didn't follow what she meant. "What?"

"I won't run away again. I won't disappear without telling you what I'm doing."

"Okay. Good," I said. If that was all I was going to get from her, then it was better than nothing. "It's getting late. Why don't we go inside?" My stomach was tight, and my head was a swirling mess. I didn't want to be caught off guard outside if Bull showed up before we were ready.

Eve stood. "Owen."

"Yeah?"

"I don't know what it will look like, and the only promise I can make right now is that I won't run, but I want to be with you," she said. "I love you.'

She loved me? I opened my mouth to ask what that meant to her, but I never got the chance. One of my MASK unit teammates appeared next to the house. "We got a visual, Alpha," he called out. "Bull is twenty miles from here."

EVE

$\mathcal{I}$nside Owen's house I sat in front of the fireplace. In my lap, I cradled an M-16. I didn't like it as a weapon, but at that moment, I needed something easier than a knife or a bow.

Owen professed his love for me, and I had just declared my love for him.

Somehow, despite our soul-baring conversation, the tension between us had rocketed up about fifty million degrees.

Owen stood near the door, but not in front of it, in case Bull had a sniper outside. He held a similar gun in his hands. Neither of us had spoken.

We should be in the bed, celebrating our new love, but here we were, holding powerful guns, with tension stabbing at us like needles.

"I wasn't going to take the job," I said. I'd seriously considered it, before I reconnected with Owen. Chicago would have been one step farther away from my previous life as a shifter; moving would have been another way to sever ties with my past.

Owen had been right. There wasn't any type of shifter life there. No clans, no community, nothing. I'd have an easier time ignoring that I'd ever been anything but human.

The job had been a good one, and it would have boosted my career. But the main draw had been the disconnect from my old life.

With a loud snap, Owen's comm crackled to life. Within a second, both of us had our guns up and ready to fire. I sagged a little when I realized it was his teammate checking in.

"Alpha," his teammate's voice boomed, "Bull's been spotted ten miles from here. Seems to heading in the exact direction."

"Thanks Brian," Owen said. "Stick to the plan."

When the comm was silent again, Owen and I moved the furniture. Owen directed me in how to make the best defensive areas to crouch behind if our play went off-script, and I ended up in a shootout.

The real plan was for me to be on the front porch, pretending to work, using my scent to ensnare Bull.

While Owen scanned the yard, I dragged a fan out onto the porch where I'd already left a laptop and some legal pads. I was going to type on the computer and make case notes, and appear to be unguarded.

I doubted Bull would think I was truly alone, but we had to start somewhere.

According to Owen, my scent was still intoxicating to an Alpha. I'd aim the fan directly where I was sitting, and hope that it helped Bull pinpoint exactly where I was.

During the week, Owen's team had gotten some potent scent blockers and suppressants, and they'd all triple dosed themselves last night. The lack of their scents created a hole in my mind, an absence where they should be. I didn't like it.

I'd grown to rely on Owen's juniper scent.

I sat down on the top porch step. I did my best not to

glance in the direction of the woods where Owen was waiting.

I cracked the laptop open and began jotting notes on a legal pad. The fan ruffled my hair as I worked. It would have been nice if Owen and I'd had more time to sort through our feelings before Bull arrived, but he'd forced our hand.

"You better live through this," I muttered to myself. After days of wading through our messy relationship, I was too close to having everything I wanted. I refused to let anyone -- even Bull -- screw this up for me.

OWEN

Hiding in the woods, watching Eve use herself as bait? Fucking torture. Why had I agreed to this? No Alpha let his omega put herself in danger. Was she my omega? Maybe not in the way I wanted. But she was close enough.

My bear insisted. *She's yours. Go get her.*

I crept to the edge of the porch. "Eve. Come on. We don't have to do this. He's on his way."

"Owen," she hissed.

"Come out here. Let me and my guys handle it." Her being up there on the porch, out in the open, didn't make a lick of sense.

Her eyes flashed. For the first time ever, she growled at me. "I am not moving. And if you try to make me, you will regret it."

I had no doubt about that. It was true, I had promised her I'd stick with the plan and let her dangle herself as bait in front of a psychopathic shifter. My bear had not made any such promises. "The second something goes fucking sideways, my bear is showing up, with or without my permission. Just so you know."

"You agreed to this plan," she said. She slashed her arm through the air. "Stick to it."

I gripped the handle of my sharpest knife. "We'll see."

Eve leaned forward to stare at me. Fury seethed from her eyes, all of it directed right at me. "You are driving me crazy," she said.

"Somehow, I know exactly what that feels like." I gave her one last look. "Be careful."

I went back to my station and adjusted my gear.

The plan was for Eve to let herself be captured. It had been her idea, based on the fact that Bull wanted her alive, to have her as one of his mates. Eve came up with the plan, and the rest of my team had agreed with her.

I was the only one who protested. But because I was on thin ice with Eve, I gave in.

I never gave in. I was the Alpha. I wasn't supposed to. Unless Eve was involved, apparently.

My team thought that once Bull felt he had won, and succeeded in getting the omega who had bested him, that he'd be distracted, let his guard down, and we could make our move.

Our intel said he was only traveling with two guards. Overpowering the three of them should have been no challenge for my team; but as we all knew, during a mission, things could go south in a split second.

We'd run through possible scenarios a few times, including ones where Bull had more than two guards, they had more weapons, or they showed up with law enforcement officers that had been bribed into aiding criminals. We talked through each one and argued about solutions.

All that prep didn't matter. I didn't feel any better about letting Eve put herself in the line of fire.

Not that I was *letting* her do anything. I could feel the scowl that had become part of my face today.

I was supposed to stand here and let Bull Payne put his disgusting hands on Eve.

My comm buzzed. "He's here."

My team was right, there he was. Bull melted out of the shadow of the woods. He came forward, taking deliberate steps. He didn't look around. He didn't look behind him. His eyes were anchored to Eve. The two guards he had with him stayed hidden in the woods.

"Eve Johnson. Hello again," Bull said.

Eve's heart rate shot up, but outwardly, she looked just as composed as ever. Bull would be able to hear her heart pounding too.

"Bull Payne," Eve said. She glanced up at him and then went back to her legal pad. Her writing never paused. "Looks like Denver County Jail fell down on its job."

"You don't seem surprised to see me," he drawled.

"I've tried a lot of cases in a big city." Eve gave a half shrug. "Not much surprises me now."

I fucking hated this, but again, I had to admit that Eve would have been an amazing soldier. She'd be an asset to any team.

"You grew up in the shifter world," Bull took a step closer to her. "You know better than to try to put me away." He took another step closer. "I'm one of your own."

My knife was harder to grip as my claws threatened to bust out of my hand. I'd never had trouble controlling my bear -- until now.

"I left that life behind," Eve said.

"Yet you smell like omega," Bull said. He took one step closer. Now he was close enough to touch her. "You smell like you're going to be mine."

A snarl rose my throat.

"I'm not going anywhere with you," Eve said.

Bull reached out and put his hand on her arm. He wasn't big for a shifter, but he was stronger than Eve. "You most certainly will. I'll show you what you've been missing while you've been playing human, while you've been trying to subvert your own kind," he said. His wrapped his fingers around her wrist and squeezed.

Eve didn't make a sound, but I saw her press her lips together to keep from crying out.

Instinct took over. Without a conscious decision, I dropped my gear. My bear came tearing out. I raced forward, and flew onto the porch. My bear rammed into Bull, knocking him away from Eve.

Within seconds, menacing growls filled the air. Bull shifted into his bear form. Shifters burst from the woods. I didn't look up to see if they were my team, or his.

Eve was all that mattered to me.

EVE

*O*f course Owen had not stuck to the plan. I'd never expected him to. In fact, he lasted longer than I'd thought.

I stood at the edge of the yard, clasping the M-16 to my chest. I hadn't shifted, not for this. I'd ducked around the side of the cabin, and I'd been ready to shoot Bull or his shifters.

Four of Owen's team ripped out of the woods to meet Bull's guards, each of them shifted into bears. Two of them, Brian and John, remained human, decked out in full Army gear.

Owen's team made quick work of the two guards, but they left Owen to deal with Bull alone.

It must have been some kind of respect thing I'd never understand. I recalled snippets of rules like that from my childhood -- rules about how and when to interfere with a fight. Apparently stepping in at the wrong time was a grave insult in some clans.

That was just more of the prehistoric crap I hadn't been willing to deal with. If I ever saw our clan again, I'd get to see up close if Owen really had gotten them to modernize a little bit.

Owen and Bull continued to grapple. Owen was a skilled fighter. The only problem was that Bull didn't seem to feel any pain. Each time Owen bit him, or swiped him with his claws, Bull didn't react.

Each time I lifted the gun to aim at Bull, he and Owen traded spots. I was a good shot, but not that good.

"Help him," I shouted to one of his teammates.

"We were ordered not to," the other said, distress clear when his voice cracked.

"Well I wasn't." Owen was winning, but there was no reason for him to end up half-dead because of some macho bullshit. "Here. Take this." I shoved the gun at John. "If you won't help, I will."

"Eve," he pleaded. He pushed the gun back into my hands. "Please. If Bull gets the upper hand, we'll step in. Owen wouldn't want you to…"

"I do not give a shit what games he's playing. I'm helping, whether any of you like it or not."

John couldn't totally hide the miniscule flinch. He was a nice guy, and I'd feel bad except Owen clearly hadn't minded sacrificing *himself* for this kill.

It was profoundly stupid for Owen to order his team not to kill Bull. But on the other hand, I understood on a visceral level why Owen wanted to be the one to kill him. Because I wanted the same thing. I didn't want to take that satisfaction from Owen, but I'd also like for Bull to die at my hand.

I'd like to know I kept any other omega from the fate he had planned for me.

"Shit," I said as two more of Bull's shifters burst from the woods, both in human form.

Our intel had been faulty. He had two additional shifters

with him, and one held what looked like a sniper rifle. Bull's shifter aimed the rifle at Owen and pulled the trigger.

I screamed as Owen hit the ground. Ice spread through my veins. Every part of me went numb, but I held tight to the gun. I got the scope to my eye, and I pulled the trigger. I hit one of Bull's guys, but not the other. The remaining one dropped to his belly, aiming the rifle at Owen's teammates too, pulling the trigger three more times. I couldn't tell if they were hit.

John stayed with me, and Brian went after Bull's shifter.

John got his arm around me. "You aren't going over there. That wasn't a bullet."

Like hell I wasn't. I tried to shake him off. "What was it?" I asked.

John didn't answer. He held tight to my upper arm. "Stay here. I'll go get him."

I let my muscles go lax. Then I waited until he loosened his grip.

As we stared at Owen lying on the ground, he transformed back into human. He'd be much easier to kill as a human. "Fuck," John said.

I bolted.

"Eve!" he shouted after me.

I got to Owen before John could snag me again. I dropped next to Owen. As I tried to think through our options, he woke up. "Eve. Go." Still lying on the ground, he shoved at my legs.

I shook his shoulders. "Owen. Stop it! Where are you hit?"

"It was another dart. But it wasn't a tranq. It made me shift back to human. Makes us easier targets."

He rolled to his side. He grabbed my hand. "Come on. I'm getting you back in the cabin. Stay low."

Near us, Brian appeared, his gun pointed toward the woods. "I've got you covered, Alpha."

We made it back inside. Once we were in, Brian and John stood outside on either side of the cabin. There was no word from their other teammates. "Stay away from the windows," Owen barked.

"What now?" I asked.

Owen pulled on a pair of pants. "They can force a turn. They've weaponized it. Medics carry small doses, but this is the first time I've seen it used in a fight. It's smart." He kicked the door. "Dammit."

"Do we have any?" I asked Owen.

"Brian should. He's the medic on our team."

"We need to get it from him. We might need it."

"Good idea." Owen used his comm to tell Brian to come to the door. Once Brian was there, he told him to hand over the shot and Owen tucked it into his jeans. "Never thought I'd have to fight with a needle." He ran his hand down my arm. "We have to get you out of here."

I didn't bother protesting. We both knew I wasn't leaving. "Escaping is not good enough. We have to get rid of Bull," I said. "I'll shift. We'll let him shoot me with the meds. I'll pretend to be passed out, and then you can move in."

"Eve, I am not risking you like that." Owen's eyes were hard. "If they hit you with a dart, you'll be stuck as a human for who knows how long. I can't shift. I'm still trying, and I fucking *can't*. I don't know how long it's going to be before it wears off."

"Owen. I love you. I respect you. But we are out of options. I'm going to shift, and I'm going after Bull. If he hits me with the dart, then use this against him." I patted his pocket where the needle was hidden. I handed him my gun. "It's full of ammo."

"Eve." He closed his eyes. "Please be careful." He gave me a hard kiss on the mouth. "I'm not going to radio my team in case Bull's hacked us."

Owen's face was blank as I ditched my clothes and shifted into my bear form. He held the door open for me. I squeezed through and stepped onto the porch. I felt Owen's hand rake through my fur.

I leaped off the porch. My bear let out a crashing roar. No shifters were visible except Bull, who stood at the edge of the woods, in human form.

"Eve. There's no need to fret," Bull said. "You'll see we've already won." He lifted his hand. From the corner of my eye, I spotted the same shifter with the rifle.

I barrelled directly toward Bull. Soon enough, I felt a sting in my shoulder. They'd hit me. I kept going, only stumbling as my four legs turned to two. I hit the ground with my face.

I never passed out completely. When I pushed myself onto my back, Bull was leaning over me.

I bared my teeth, fully aware it didn't have the same effect when I was human.

A bullet whizzed by. It struck Bull in the shoulder. He fell backward and hit the ground, but it didn't slow him for long.

"Stay down!" Owen shouted at me.

Bull got to his knees. Blood rushed down his arm, but a slow grin stretched across his face. "Eve. We'll be together soon," he said. Then he shifted into his bear.

Owen ran straight at him, firing his gun, but Bull didn't stop. He had to be jacked up on a massive amount of drugs. In human form, even armed, Owen was no match for a five-hundred pound bear who wasn't feeling pain.

And neither was I. I had no weapons with me, but I got up and trudged toward them. We couldn't stop until Bull was dead.

Bull roared in Owen's face before swiping his claws across his chest. Owen toppled backward, and I lurched forward, trying to grab him. We fell together.

I got my hand in his back pocket and grabbed the shot he'd stashed there. With me in the way, Bull didn't attack Owen, but as soon as I moved away, Bull was so busy trying to rip Owen's head off that he didn't notice me get close to his ribs. I raised my arm and rammed the needle full of medicine into his skin.

Within seconds, Bull was back to human. Blood rushed from his mouth, but he kept grinning at me. "Eve," he said.

I jumped on him, pinning his shoulders down with my hands. Owen crawled forward. He sank his knife into Bull's neck, right over his throat.

Then Owen passed out.

Bull was dead.

I should be thrilled, except I wasn't, because Owen was lying on the ground covered in blood. I ran my hand over his forehead. There was so much blood that I couldn't tell where he was injured.

"Hey Owen, Bull's dead. You killed him," I said, scared to touch him in any of the places where Bull had mauled him.

I hoped he could hear me. One of his soldiers dropped a thick blanket over my shoulders, and another blanket over Owen. I looked up to see that it was John. "Thanks," I mumbled. The night air would be chilly soon.

Owen didn't move.

"Eve, you know Brian is a medic," John said. "He can help if it's okay with you. He can give Owen something for the pain, and we can get him inside." They waited, obviously anxious to save their Alpha, but unwilling to go against my wishes.

They were already deferring to me as if I were his mate. Had he said something to them? Or was this just based on their observations of what they thought he'd want?

"Yes." I pulled the blanket tighter around my shoulders. "Please. Do whatever you can to help him."

In a flurry of motion, three of Owen's teammates knelt beside him. I crawled back and sat on the ground, still wearing the blanket. My clothes were somewhere close by, but I didn't care.

If Owen could survive this, then we were free. The chaos was over. Without their master, Bull's followers would scatter. The ones we could find would be arrested, and charged. Others would escape, but none had his ability to pull the strings of a massive criminal organization. They'd only been able to obey his orders.

I could go back home. To Denver. I absolutely would not be taking the job in Chicago. It was a no-brainer at this point. I wouldn't leave Owen, and I wouldn't ask him to give up his entire life to live in a place he'd loathe.

If they truly needed me in Chicago, I could fly out for a few weeks and then work on the research from Colorado. It had taken me thirty years to accept having Owen in my life. I wasn't going to screw that up now because of a job.

I only hoped I'd get the chance to tell him that.

OWEN

With great effort, I forced my eyes to open. I was lying on the ground, in human form, with my teammates bent over me. They were all talking, to each other and to me, but I couldn't make out the words. I felt the prick of a needle in my arm several times, the scrape of scissors, the rattle of packages being opened.

Eve. Where was Eve? I tried to roll to my side, but I couldn't make any part of my body cooperate. One of my teammates pushed me back down. I couldn't focus well enough to see who it was. "Alpha, don't move," he said.

"Eve," I said. I wanted to shout, but my voice was a hoarse whisper. "Where is she?"

They still didn't answer me. I got one arm up and grabbed my teammate around the neck. He swatted my hand away and pressed my arm back down. "Sorry Alpha. But you have to be still while they do these stitches."

I didn't fucking care about that. Had something happened to Eve? Was she hurt?

Eve!

I got my head turned to the side. Even that took effort.

My heart clenched in relief. Eve was about twenty feet away, bent over Bull's bloody body.

I watched as she lifted a knife over her head and drove it into his chest. He was dead, I remembered that much. I'd gotten him down on the ground when Eve had joined me. She'd helped pin him to the ground, and I'd ripped out his throat.

I'd listened as Bull's heart had slowed, then stopped. Why was she stabbing him? If he could recover from what I'd done to him, we had a bigger problem on our hands.

"Eve." My voice was sluggish, but this time it actually made noise.

Her head whipped toward me. "Owen!" She left the knife in Bull's chest and ran toward me. John moved over to make room for her as she dropped to her knees beside me. "You're awake."

"Bull's dead?" I asked, gasping the words. Everything hurt. Now that I knew Eve was safe, the adrenaline faded, and I felt every gash.

"Yes. He's dead. You killed him." She put her hand on my head. "But I had to make sure."

I understood that. The knife in the heart had been for her own peace of mind. Her own closure.

I knew then, I wasn't letting her go. If she wanted to take the job in Chicago, I'd go with her. I'd hate the city, but I'd be with Eve. I could find a place to shift every now and then, and I'd make it work.

As I made the decision, my bear hummed as though he'd been fed salmon and steak at once. He liked clear decisions. The bear didn't care about nuance, or what I might sacrifice. He wanted me with my mate, and that was final.

Leaving my MASK team would feel like tearing myself in half, but for my mate, I'd do it gladly. I could always visit them.

Could I live a human's life? It was likely another shifter unit would want me to work for them, probably doing undercover work in the city. Military shifters were rare enough that the units were always eager for more -- as long as I was active for duty, I'd have a job. Undercover work wasn't my favorite, but I would try. Maybe it wouldn't be forever. Eve could boost her career, then we could come back to Denver.

Letting her go alone was not an option. My bear would never watch her walk away again without urging me to do all I could to make sure we were together.

Eve had given me a second chance with her. She'd had to give up her life once before. This time, I could man up and be the one to make a change.

"Is he going to make it?" I asked John as quietly as I could. After I'd spoken to Owen, I'd tried to get out of the soldiers' way while they were treating Owen's wounds, but Owen had grabbed my hand. He didn't want me to go.

"He should be fine. He'll feel a lot better by morning," John said. "He'll be back on active duty in a week."

I sagged. My head dropped forward, and I covered my face with my hand. I didn't have the energy to cry.

Owen would live.

After treating his wounds, Owen's soldiers carried him inside. They all survived the attack, thank God. They all stayed overnight, surrounding the cabin, still watching.

I stayed with Owen for the first few hours, afraid to leave him. But as the hours wore on, his breathing remained steady, so I snuck away to shower and eat. While I was in the kitchen, I peeked outside to see one of the MASK soldiers standing on the porch, scanning the yard, protecting us.

These were Owen's teammates, as close to him as family. I didn't want to hinder their bond in any way. I stepped outside. I recognized John, and I wanted to let him know how much I appreciated him, and the rest of the team. "Thank you," I said. "For everything. I know you and Owen are close, so even though I'm here, please feel free to use the shower, bathroom, kitchen. Whatever you need."

"We're fine out here." He smiled. "We're glad to see the Alpha happy."

I didn't want to know if he knew about my history with Owen. I figured a fresh start was best. "Can I at least bring you some food?"

John nodded. "We'll never turn down food."

In the kitchen, I made piles of sausage, eggs and bacon for the team. The team inhaled the meal, and by the time I was done cleaning up, I heard water running. I rushed into the bathroom to find Owen in the shower. "Hey! Should you be up?"

He pulled the curtain aside to smile at me. "I'm fine. Alphas heal even faster than normal shifters."

Unconvinced, I waited in the bathroom until Owen stepped out, holding a towel. He did look much better, although dark purple bite marks still marred his ribs. Across his chest, the claw marks were present, but healing.

Despite the still-healing wounds, his body was still just as hot as ever. I wanted to touch him. I lifted one hand, and reached out to touch his still-damp chest. Then my eyes spotted the stitches in his shoulder. I yanked my hand back. I had no business touching him until he was well.

He grabbed my hand in his. "Eve."

I blinked as he took a slow step toward me. Before I knew it, he leaned in and mouthed at my neck. "I saw you looking at me," he said.

I moaned as his lips skimmed my jaw. "I don't want to hurt you," I breathed.

"It would hurt if you didn't touch me."

I opened my eyes to see the crooked smile on his face. "That was corny. I was really turned on, and now I'm trying not to laugh."

"It's true though. I want you to touch me."

"Are you sure?"

He lifted his eyebrows and gestured downward. "Doesn't it look like I'm sure?"

I wrapped my arms around him carefully, very aware of his hardness pressed between us.

He gave me a quick kiss on the mouth. "Are you okay?" He held my face in his hands. "Were you injured at all?"

"Not one bit."

"Thank God." He leaned his forehead against mine, a gesture I'd watched him do many times before. It had seemed sweet when we were kids, now it seemed poignant. I didn't ever want to take it for granted.

"I don't know what I'd have done," he said. "I don't want to live without you anymore." He exhaled quickly. "It's not easy for me to be upfront about my feelings," he said, the words spilling out. "I'd rather say nothing. But after what you've been through, I want you to know."

He'd been through just as much as I had, and then some. "I don't want to live without you either."

His hands dropped down to cup my backside. His lips skimmed over my cheek. "Are you okay with this right now?"

I nodded. I heard what he wasn't saying: *I need you.* I needed him too.

"Do you know how much I want you," he asked.

"I think I have an idea."

"I like you in my clothes," he said. "But I want you naked. Let's get you undressed," he said.

I pulled off the t-shirt and sweatpants of his that I was wearing. He kissed me, stepping backward and walking me to the bed.

He smoothed his hands over my hair. "You are amazing."

"You're pretty awesome yourself."

"Are you sure you're feeling okay enough for this?" Owen's injuries wouldn't scare me off, but I hated the thought of him being in pain for this.

"I feel great," he said. "I feel a lot better than I look." He ran his hands down my spine. "Any requests?"

"I want you to take what you need." I blinked, a little shocked I'd gotten the words out. I meant every word. But who'd have thought I'd ever speak those words to a male?

"You are the best thing that's ever happened to me. Then, and now," he said.

I prided myself on not being sentimental or emotional. But Owen's words sliced through any barriers I had left. His honesty was refreshing, and I wanted to make him happy. "Tell me what you want," I insisted.

Owen's growl rumbled low in his chest. "Turn around. Lie face down on the bed. I need to see this lovely bottom."

My blood sizzled. I never thought I'd like being spoken to so frankly. When the words came from Owen, I loved it. I did as he asked. I lay across the bed, with my chest pressed flat against the mattress. "Your bottom is the perfect height for me like this."

He stood behind me, caressing my backside. He parted my folds with one hand while he rubbed his erection against me. "I had you from behind during your heat. But I didn't get the chance to really slow down and enjoy the sight," he said. "Push your knees apart. Spread your legs."

I hesitated. What must I look like? I didn't look like other omegas. Sure, we'd done this during my heat, but I didn't have clear memories of it. And sex during a heat was different. Heat sex was lust-fueled and somewhat mindless. This was careful, deliberate, and planned.

I was confident in myself, and at peace with my non-omega like body, but putting it on display like this was another thing altogether.

"Eve? Is something wrong?" Owen asked.

I was not going to whine about my curvy backside to Owen after he'd almost been killed by the shifter who was stalking me. No way. "No, I'm fine."

"If you want to stop, we stop. But if you're just feeling shy, then let me assure you that I want you more than words can express." Owen kissed my shoulder blade, then my spine. "I don't know if you care what I think, but in case you do, you are the hottest, sexiest, most stunning female I've ever seen." He crawled up to breathe the words against my neck. "And seeing you like this makes me want to explode."

After a speech like that, no fucking way did I want to stop. If he said he liked looking, then I'd take his word for it. I was turned on now, a heated fire coursing its way through my body, concentrated between my legs, where the arousal made me ache for Owen. "I want you too, Owen. Don't stop." I was grateful to hear him open a packet. Owen would be a great dad, but I wasn't ready for that.

"Alpha. Please." It felt good to call him Alpha, and I wanted him more than any words could say. I needed him to fill me up. Maybe one day soon I'd be able to say the graphic words out loud to him, when I wasn't in the throes of a heat. If we stayed together and became mated, we'd have this every day. Not just the sex, although it was incredible. But we'd have the closeness, and the companionship. I hadn't known what I was missing.

But now that I'd had a taste of Owen in my life, I didn't want to go back to living without him.

Owen's chest rumbled with growl of pleasure. "I love it when you call me Alpha. I wish you could see this. Next time we're getting a mirror," he said, voice gritty as he pushed into me.

"Owen!" I cried out in shock at the suggestion. A mirror? Six months ago, I'd never have agreed to seeing myself exposed like this. But with Owen, I was intrigued, and I might just get there one day. I arched my back, vaguely recalling him saying he liked that during my heat.

Folded over on my knees, with my head down and my bottom up, I'd never felt more like an omega.

It was a position I'd never thought I'd accept, yet during my heat, I craved it. Now that I was aware enough to consider it, I savored the feeling of Owen behind me, and inside me.

It was no secret that this was the position shifter mates used during their first time, and when they wanted to conceive. I wasn't sure if Owen chose this on purpose, or if instinct was driving him. It didn't matter whether he chose it or not, because how he felt was clear.

I had to let him know I was ready to accept him as a mate, though this wasn't the right time. This moment was for expressing the raw, primal connection between us. I had to tell him soon; I didn't want to wait another day to let him know I wanted him -- not just as a human boyfriend, but as a permanent partner, one that was loyal for life.

I had to tell him I wanted him as my mate.

OWEN

Last night, I thought I was going to die. And for a moment, I'd been terrified I'd lost Eve.

But now, we were together in my bed. I'd told her to bend forward on the bed and get on her knees, and to my surprise, she'd done as I asked.

She'd laid her naked body out for me, with her backside presented for me. As I pushed my hardness into her entrance, her curvy cheeks parted for me. She opened herself to, physically and otherwise.

I thrust into her, relishing the sight of her upturned bottom. I drove into her, over and over, until the need to see her beautiful face overcame me. As hot as her round ass made me, I wanted to see her eyes, her mouth, her full lips.

I rubbed my hand down her back. "Sweetheart. Turn over."

I pulled out and helped her turn to her back. In front of me, she lay with her legs spread. Her scent soaked into my flannel sheets. No matter how much they were washed, they'd always smell of honey and spruce to me.

My bear's satisfaction strummed through my chest. When

she'd called me Alpha, my bear had nearly erupted with happiness.

"Your bottom was the perfect height." I knelt on the floor and tugged her to the edge of the bed. "But now so is your pussy," I said.

She flushed all over at my words. "I tasted you during your heat. But I need more." I ducked down to lick her sweet honeyed folds. I held tight to one of her ankles while she thrashed. I pushed two fingers into her drenched sex. I licked and sucked at her clit, unable to get enough.

"Owen! I'm close!" she yelled.

All these years, I'd gone without her. I would do anything to make this work between us. "Don't fight it."

When I'd woken up outside and hadn't seen Eve, I thought my life was over.

If Eve and I lived together, we'd have this every day. Not just sex, but love. Time together. I'd asked her to mate with me. She'd lived among humans for ten years, so marriage might mean something to her too, so we would get married if she wanted. If she accepted, we could have both a human wedding in Denver, and a shifter mating ceremony in Avon.

With my tongue licking her folds, and my fingers in her pussy, she came. Wave after wave of pleasure crested as she writhed. "Now I want you to come on me."

I crawled up on the bed. I lifted Eve and settled her against the pillows. "Comfortable?"

She nodded. "Good. Because I plan to take my time." I positioned my throbbing rod at her slick entrance. I plunged into her as she cried out. "I love you," I said.

"I love you too," she said, moaning into my ear. "But that's not all."

I stilled, hovering above her. I rose up on one elbow so I could see her pretty face. My ribs twinged as I moved, but it was worth it. I traced my thumb over her lush mouth. "Not all?"

Eve's eyes met mine. "When we talked. Earlier. When you said you loved me…" Eve swallowed hard and glanced away, breaking our eye contact.

Inside her body, I stayed hard, but my heart began to batter against my chest. Eve was gifted with words, and yet now she was struggling to finish her sentence. "What's wrong?" I asked. Surely she wouldn't tell me she was leaving right now, not while our bodies were connected. I'd survived heartbreak once. I couldn't do it again.

"Nothing." Eve squeezed her eyes shut, then opened them. This time she met my eyes, with her familiar steely gaze. "I'm only nervous."

"Tell me," I said.

Eve ran her hands over my shoulders and down my back. "I promised that I wouldn't leave again. I'm ready now. I want more. I want us to be together. I don't know what that's going to look like. We can figure it out," she said, all her words tumbling out in a rush.

My heart slowed its pounding beat, but my stomach started to swirl. "Eve. You know that I want you as my mate. Are you trying to say you want the same thing?"

She breathed out a sigh. "Yes."

"You want to be my mate?"

She lifted her hips, spurring my body to react. "Yes," she said. She wrapped her legs around my waist. I rocked forward with her smooth thighs pressed against me.

I pushed up on my hands, changing the angle so I could hit her sweet spot with each thrust. "If I wasn't already making love to you, I'd have you on your back in two seconds," I panted. I scented her, inhaling her sweet scent. "I'll go to Chicago," I said.

Under me, she writhed. "What are you talking about?"

"The job you want in Chicago." My thrusts picked up speed. I was close. "I'll go with you, if that's what you want."

"You would?" she asked.

"Without a doubt." I couldn't believe we were carrying on this conversation right now. But I was unwilling to stop either. I wanted her to come for me, and I wanted her commitment too.

Eve's breathing turned fast. She sucked in a breath as she lifted her hips to meet each thrust. "What about your job?" she ground out.

I couldn't answer that right now. Nothing mattered but what was going on in my bed. I lowered my body to press against hers. I got both my arms under Eve and held her close, still keeping most of my weight off of her. I couldn't get close enough to her as I slowed my thrusts. Rolling my hips, I pulled all the way out, then drove back in. I slid one hand down to rub between her legs.

Within seconds, Eve's body shook. Her folds spasmed intensely, drawing my own orgasm from me. As I spilled my seed, I kissed her cheek. "You're it for me, Eve. Always my mate."

"Owen. You're the same for me. It took me ten years to get here, but you are my mate."

I didn't let go of her. I rolled us to the side, and we fell asleep with my body still inside hers.

We must have slept for about an hour. I woke up long enough to pull the blanket over us. Eve snuggled into my side. "Mmm. Warm." She blinked up at me. "How are you feeling?"

Now that the endorphins from sex had worn off, as well as the industrial strength painkillers, each bite and claw mark ached, and each breath brought an insistent sting, but it was a small price to pay for having Eve in my arms, safe from that bastard. "A little beat up, but otherwise great."

"I'm so glad," she said. She sighed. "I realize that bringing up a bunch of important topics during sex probably wasn't my best idea."

"Nah." I kissed her nose. "Seemed to work out just fine."

"You didn't answer my question though."

I had no idea what question she was talking about. She said she wanted to be my mate, so I was good. At this point, I didn't have the brain power to pretend to know. "What question was that?"

She smiled. "The one about your job. How would you work in Chicago?"

Ah, that question. It was important, but not as important as Eve. "The military has bases all over the country. The shifter units are small and well-connected. I can get reassigned."

"Is that something you want? To leave? Your team here seemed like family."

"I don't want to leave." I traced my finger over the shape of her ear. Every part of her was beautiful. "My team here is family. But you're my mate. You'll be my home."

Eve sniffed. She patted her face with my sheet. "Don't make me cry. I've made it through all of this without falling apart." She grabbed my hand. "Thank you. For sticking by me. For not giving up on me."

I pressed my mouth against hers. After making out for a few minutes, she cuddled into me with a sleepy sigh, and fell asleep on my shoulder.

Once I was certain she was asleep again, I crept from the bed and pulled on some clothes. In the den, I started a fire. By the time I was done outside, the entire room should be warm. As shifters, we didn't feel cold the same way humans did, but a fire would still be cozy.

I had to find something to make a ring with. At my cabin in Avon, I had tools and woodworking supplies. Here, there was no garage, no shed -- I had only what we needed to survive.

In the kitchen pantry I found thin wire and wire cutters. I cut off three strips, and I measured the size against my own. Eve's hands weren't tiny, but they were smaller than mine, and her fingers were slim and elegant. I did my best to braid three wires together.

I crept outside. Near the edge of the cabin, I spotted John, who must have taken the night watch. My team had saved my life. And not only that, they'd accepted Eve without question, because I did, even given our rocky history together. They hadn't asked questions, they hadn't snubbed her. They'd just protected her.

"Hey Alpha," John called out. "Feeling better?"

"Much. I should have come out earlier to let you know." I gripped his arm. He and the rest weren't on duty now that Bull was dead. They'd stuck around for me, and for Eve. "Thank you. For everything."

John nodded. He could certainly tell Eve and I were in the process of mating, and he likely knew I was in a hurry to get back to her. I'd make it up to my team soon enough.

In the woods, I found a Spruce tree. I hoped I wasn't going overboard. When I was fifteen, I'd put a little sprig of spruce in everything I gave Eve. I'd even taken to dropping spruce needles on her paperwork at school, or sticking them under the windshield wipers of her car. That was the year my love for Eve had changed from friendship, to that of a mate.

Eve had always grinned, and tucked the spruce needles into her pockets. I hoped the memory was happy, and not an unpleasant reminder. The smell was spicier than Eve's gentle scent, but it would do. With my knife, I cut off a small bundle.

~

I slipped back into bed. When my frigid skin touched hers, she shivered. Shit. I'd forgotten to warm up before I hopped back in the bed. I'd been so preoccupied with getting the ring and the tree needles into an envelope that I hadn't noticed the chill. "Cold?" I asked.

She rubbed her face against the pillow. "A little."

Oh well. I'd made the perfect excuse to leave the bedroom. "I have a fire going in the den."

"Sounds perfect," she said. I lifted her, and carried her into the den where I had blankets in front of the fire. "Please be careful," she said. "Don't crack the rest of your ribs carrying me."

"Are you implying that I'm not strong enough to carry my omega?"

She grinned. "If I'm going to say something, I won't imply. I'll just say it." She gave me a big smacking kiss on the cheek. "I could get used to this," she said as I lowered her to the floor.

I really hoped she would. I would happily carry her around for the rest of our lives. I kept that thought to myself, not wanting to ruin my surprise. She wasn't wrong about my ribs, although it had nothing to do with carrying her. Bull had really done a number on me. But I would not let that bastard screw up my plans for one second.

We lay in front of the fireplace, snuggled together while I tried to suppress the panic that rolled through my stomach. "I'm not going to Chicago," she said.

"What?" Did she mean she wasn't taking the job? Had I zoned out for part of the conversation? "Why?"

"I don't want you to leave your team. I saw how you all interact. How you take care of each other. They love you, and they watch your back." She reached up and ran her hand through my hair, something she hadn't done since we were teens. "Colorado has plenty of opportunities, but I'm not ready to leave Denver yet."

"That's fine for me," I assured her. "I can work in the surrounding areas and come out here on the weekends, or whatever works for us."

Eve moved to sit on the hearth of the fireplace. "Being out here with you, and with your team, has reawakened all I loved about being a shifter. I'd like to try visiting Avon sometime. I'd like to try and see my parents, and our clan, if you think it's a good idea."

I quickly closed my jaw from where it had dropped open. I was still elated that Eve wanted to be my mate. There was no way I was going to press her about visiting our clan, but if it was her idea, I'd do everything I could to make it work. "I think it's a great idea. I think it'll go over better than you expect." I winked at her. "And if it doesn't, then I'll put them all in exile."

"Right, because you're the big powerful Alpha." Her eyes lit up as she laughed at me.

I moved to sit at Eve's side on the hearth. "Pretty much." I pressed my hand against the small envelope in my pocket. Whew. Still there.

Some of the human traditions were cool, some were nerve-wracking. Shifter mating ceremonies were much simpler. Once the couple announced their intention, everyone got together in the woods to shift and then hunt together. Once the mating couple caught something -- hopefully a deer or something large -- then the clan went back to have a moonlit picnic. Then voila, the couple was mated in the eyes of the clan.

Simple. Easy. Fast. The ring-giving the humans did was cool, but I wouldn't be able to wear one most days -- if I shifted, I'd lose it. However, if Eve kept practicing law, she'd be able to wear a ring to work.

She laughed and I pulled her in tight again. "Seriously, if it works out, great. If not, we can form a new clan, just the two of us," I said.

She turned to face me head on. "Speaking of clans. Your team treated me like your mate. Did you tell them?"

"No. I didn't say a word to them. They must have been going on instinct." Which was a perfect place for me to try this human proposal thing. Jeez. I should have watched a few of those romantic comedies my parents liked.

"Eve," I said, trying not to let my voice become oddly formal. Not only would Eve be suspicious, I'd sound like a dope. She was already staring at me with her eyebrows drawn together.

If I didn't get it together, she'd be howling with laughter before long. I licked my lips. "We've already discussed mating, and I can't tell you how happy you've made me. But I know we'll probably spend time living among humans too." I drew in a big breath.

"So," I said as I got down on one knee. "I'd like to have both traditions, if you're interested. A clan mating ceremony, and a human one. Would you marry me?" I fumbled the envelope out of my pocket and handed it to her.

"Owen." Through all of the chaos, I'd never seen Eve cry. Now she sniffed, and her eyes were wet as she pulled open the paper and found the ring. "Did you make this?"

"Yes." Something made by our own hand meant more in the shifter world than in the human.

"And these are spruce needles," she said. She pressed her

face close to the envelope and closed her eyes. "Because you've always said I smelled like honey and spruce."

I nodded. She still hadn't said yes.

She sat with her eyes closed for a few moments. She opened those bright green eyes and the corners of her lips turned up.

She placed the envelope on the hearth and flung her arms around me. "Owen Brady, I would love to marry you and be your mate."

My muscles went lax. Relief. I stood and lifted Eve into the air, spinning her around. My ribs creaked in protest. Afraid of dropping her, I sat her down quickly. I couldn't stop my gasp.

"Oh no. Owen! I'm sorry. Did that hurt?"

"It's fine," I groaned. My ribs felt like someone was prying them apart with a crowbar.

Not much was going to affect me at this moment. Eve was going to marry me. She'd be my wife. And most importantly, she'd be my mate.

EVE

I got Owen some ice for his ribs, and helped him wrap them up. He'd been so distracted after the shower and our lengthy lovemaking, that he hadn't taken care of himself at all. "You already asked me to be your mate," I said.

"Yes," he said, still taking shallow breaths.

"And now you asked me to marry you."

"Yes."

"Do you mean in a legally-binding, human way? With paperwork?" In the clan world, matings didn't come with paperwork. A record was made by one of the elders, and the Alpha kept a list, but no one signed a paper. Making it legal was of little consequence, since the pairing was for life.

"Yes again. That's exactly what I meant."

"That is wonderful." I cupped Owen's jaw and kissed him. "Do you think you can walk outside?"

"Sure. Where are we going?"

"Come on." I wanted to share the news. And I wanted to share it with shifters first. I'd lost all my relationships with shifters when I left, but now I could start to rebuild that bridge with Owen's crew. "Let's tell your team!"

"Right now?" Owen looked sideways at me. "I mean, I'm sure they'll be happy for us, but they can wait."

I knew how much he valued his team. Why was he being so weird? "Do you not want to tell anyone?"

"Eve. Of course I do. I thought we'd have a little time alone first."

Ah. "Were you hoping for some celebratory sex?" I spotted the pink blush spreading across his face. "You are!"

Owen had the grace to look sheepish. "Can you blame me?"

"I think I can. You're black and blue, and you're feeling it today, even though you don't want to admit it." I stood on my tiptoes. I would never get tired of how good it felt to be smaller than my mate. My husband. "Alpha," I said. "I promise you we'll get to celebrate."

He rubbed the back of his neck where it was still flushing bright red.

"But for now," I said. "Let's tell your team. You may think they don't care, but I swear to you, they do. I saw them when we thought you might die."

He caught my arm and wrapped his strong fingers around my wrist. "I'm sorry," he said.

"No need to be sorry."

"I wish you hadn't had to see that."

"I'm glad I did. I know they have your back when you're out there." Their calm competence had gotten us all through the night. I took his hand, and we stepped onto the porch.

"John!" I called out. "We have good news." I nudged Owen, careful not to hit him in the ribs.

He cleared his throat before speaking to John. "I asked Eve to marry me in a human ceremony. She said yes. And she has agreed to be my mate."

John beamed at his Alpha, then at me. "Congratulations!" he said. "Will you be going to Avon soon?"

"Maybe in a few weeks," Owen said. "We'll need to go back to Denver, and check on Eve's house, and she'll go back to work now that Bull's taken care of."

In that moment, I knew I didn't want to delay our visit to Avon. It would only make it harder on both of us. "Thank you, John," I said. I tugged at Owen's hand, and we stepped off the porch into the yard. "I'm ready now," I said.

I'd lived my life on my own terms for ten years. I'd faced a monster, and I'd been forced to kill other shifters to survive. In the middle of all of that, I'd found my mate again. I could absolutely handle my family and my clan.

"For what?"

"To go to Avon."

Owen frowned. "There's no rush."

"I want to start our life together. That means seeing my family, talking to the clan."

He rubbed his hands up and down my arms. "If you say you're ready, then I trust you." He pressed his lips against mine for a long second. "Eve. You are the best thing that's ever happened to me. Then, and now. Whatever happens in Avon won't affect our life together, because I won't let it. You are my mate, and I love you."

I wrapped my arms around his waist tipped my head up to kiss him. "We'll figure it out together," I said. "We made it work after ten years apart, so we can do anything. You're my mate, and my Alpha."

"And you're my Omega," Owen said.

For the first time, I was thrilled to hear those words.

He's mine, my bear insisted. My bear could rest easy -- I wasn't going to let him go this time.

"I love you too," I said. I couldn't resist saying it one more time, "Let's get going, Alpha."

WANT TO KEEP THE MAGIC GOING? CHECK OUT REAPER'S OF CRESCENT CITY

REAPER'S MARK

PROLOGUE

A bead of sweat trickled down Axel's temple. Heavy, sweltering heat weighed upon him as he rowed through the thick waters of the bayou. *They can't get me now,* Axel chanted feverishly under his breath. His flashlight pierced through the fog, casting a shaky path in the darkness.

"They can't..." Axel's heart leapt to his throat. "Get your claws off me, you slimy son of a bitch!"

The pale, spindly hand latched onto his pirogue undaunted, taunting even. Grabbing his dagger, Axel let spill a string of profanities, including the odd *"putain"* from his childhood. It had been years since he had cussed in Cajun French – but then it had been years since he had been here in the swamps, battling some grisly creature of the dark.

Without a second's hesitation, Axel whacked the monster's hand off. Only he was met with little more resistance than air. Inspecting the familiar greenery that was entangled on his blade, a wave of embarrassment washed over him. Here he was, a sturdy, grown man of nearly forty five, waging war against some Spanish moss. Maybe not so much had changed since he was a Rougarou-fearing boy on the bayou after all.

With a huff, Axel tossed the scraggly plant away. Of all the places to be after the sun went down… *You better be right this time around, you crazy old pirate, or your next two hundred years are going to be dry as a bone,* Axel thought to himself mercilessly. The mental image of pouring all Pierre St. Patin's rum down the Mississippi already brought an evil smile to his lips.

Still, he squinted in the dark, trying to spot something that may even remotely look like a tombstone. This was the most precise information the pirate ghost had given him in years. Axel had spent many nights listening to the old mercenary's long, drunken rants. Jumbled tales of being at sea, virgin islands and beautiful girls – in particular his long-lost mistress Adelaide, a runaway slave girl the pirate had loved and lost to smallpox.

"She was lovely," Pierre St. Patin had choked over his glass of rum a couple weeks ago at the Last Barrel Bar. "So lovely I put her in the ground with a mirror so the lass could gaze at her loveliness forever."

The romantic moment was broken when the pirate ghost snorted, sending phantom droplets of alcohol flying everywhere. "And a fat lot of good that does to her, staring at the worms eating at her skull all day. Meanwhile, I was six feet above, breathing and poor as Job's turkey. Tellin' you, that damned mirror was worth all the sugar in the Caribbean."

Axel had eyed his drinking buddy with skepticism. Not one for romance himself, he asked: "Well, couldn't you just dig it back out?"

Pierre banged his glass against the table. "I tried! I tried my damnedest best to get my hands back on that coffin. But every time I tried, I bloody near met my death. Until I did."

Turning to Axel with more lucidity in his see-through eyes than ever before, the pirate muttered: "Aye, it was like the wench's grave was cursed."

That caught Axel's attention. "Do you think it could've been more than just a mirror? That it could've held some sort of magick?"

But by then, Pierre had veered off on some tall tale about dueling the Kraken.

Questions travel far. Which was why two weeks and a few hangovers later, Axel was at the place in the world he least wanted to be: the wetlands where he and his Grandma Tabby had lived nearly three decades ago. A muggy, forsaken place fit for monsters. Alligators and black widows were the least of his worries. Beasts with glowing red eyes, claws long as his finger, teeth sharper than a blade, large thrashing wings and –

His boat shook. Violently. Before Axel could wonder if he had bumped into a tree or something of the kind, the pirogue rocked so hard it threatened to topple over. Gripping his trusty dagger once again, he backed away just in time to avoid a heavy tail whacking him in the face.

He only caught a glimpse of the creature that leapt from the water, but it was enough. Axel's heart stilled. A hefty, powerful silhouette covered with scales. Long, ratty strands hanging from a few scraggly patches of hair.

Axel knew what this monster was. Any Cajun would know. Though he had only ever heard about it through Grandma Tabby's tales, there was no mistaking the unholy union between an ape and an alligator. Right then, Axel Lacroix was facing a Letiche. The worst nightmare of any poor soul trying to make their way through the bayou.

The swamp monster attacked again, landing a mighty thump that had Axel falling on the floor. He crawled back up and jabbed his dagger blindly, but the Letiche was too far out of his reach.

There was a moment's calm. Axel clutched his flashlight with clammy hands and shone a beam on the swamp. After all the commotion, a grim silence had settled. Long grasses swayed with the current, much like the Letiche's hair. Craggy bits of wood that looked like the beast's scaly skin bobbed up and down.

Then all of a sudden, surging from deep below, an incredibly strong blow sent the pirogue flying into the air. It fell back upside down.

This is it, were the words that echoed through Axel's mind as he flailed blindly underwater. *This time, your hour is up.* He was going to die, he realized. His arms fumbled to find the surface, but all they met was the hard wood of the overturned boat. He was running out of air. He felt the Letiche swishing nearby.

He was going to die, but it wouldn't be in his lavish mansion in New Orleans. He wouldn't be surrounded by beautiful women. No, Axel would die in the bayous where he had grown up. And all he would have for company was a smelly swamp monster. He actually kind of snorted, which didn't help his current situation at all.

But it's not fair if you die now, came the little voice in Axel's head as the rest of him was closing down. *You were a dirt poor kid in a cabin, and look where you ended up! You're rich, and you have so many of them all under your thumb.* Axel's mind went to the supernaturals back in town that were at his mercy – Hippolyte the starved vampire, even the rogue ghost Pierre St. Patin. *All you need is this mirror they all want*, the greedy voice continued to whisper, *and you'll have them all in your pocket. You can't die now. It's not fair...*

And then he made it to the surface. Finally, Axel gasped for air. He couldn't let go. He just wasn't wired that way. And he was so close. So close to tightening the reins on supernaturals for good, until they could barely breathe. They deserved no better, after breathing down his neck during his whole childhood.

The Letiche chose that moment to burst through the water again, a mass of lethal power covered in hair and leaves. It snapped its jaw. Axel wasn't the frailest of humans, but he would be little more than a toothpick if he were caught between that beast's teeth.

Out of pure instinct, Axel threw himself with as much force as he could muster onto the overturned boat. Almost as if it were in slow-motion, he watched the front side shoot up in counterbalance. The Letiche craned its neck, shaking its scraggly mane and sending droplets all over. Then the pointed end of the pirogue struck hard on the beast's sensitive, exposed underjaw.

A deafening roar sliced through the silence of the night. Then the mutant's colossal body went limp. Axel was plunged underwater again, carried into the vortex of the monster's fall.

When he made his way back up again, heaving and heart beating furiously, Axel saw something that brought a smile back to his quivering lips. Over in the distance, floating above the veil of fog, a blue orb glowed eerie in the dark.

A *fifolet*. Strange balls of light known to blaze deep in the swamps, showing the way to forgotten treasures. Axel crawled back onto his upended pirogue, ready to lay hands on Adelaide's cursed mirror.

ARLA

"*N*o he did *not!*" Arla cried in a rare fit of outrage. "The jackass! That depraved, greedy, blockheaded…"

She ran out of words insulting enough as she took in the details of the vile human's crimes. When she reached the end of the letter, she shakily folded it back into the envelope and passed a weary hand over her eyes.

Axel Lacroix.

The name made her heart burn with such spite it could have warmed even the Devil's feet. Trying to hold herself from performing black magick on the spot, Arla trudged over to her desk and opened a drawer none too gently. She tossed the envelope inside, where it joined a myriad of other envelopes that looked just like it – all sealed with the same star-shaped symbol and the initials O.M.A.

It was hardly the first time the Order of Magickal Affairs contacted her on the subject of Axel Lacroix. The over-flowing drawer dedicated entirely to the infuriating man was proof of that.

Whatever had inspired the mortal to wreak havoc in

supernatural affairs the moment he had set foot in New Orleans, she did not know. Most non-magickal humans led pretty tame, inoffensive lives, far from the businesses of creatures of the night. Arla should know. Caught between the wars of the two most powerful beings, vampires and werewolves, it was her job both as a mortal and as a witch to protect innocent humans.

She snorted. Innocent wasn't a word she would use in any proximity with this lowlife's name though. It seemed half of her job as a supervisor of local magickal matters was spent dealing with Axel Lacroix's offenses.

We the Fae of the Botanical Gardens hereby declare the activities of Axel Lacroix and his ghost tour unendurable. Our delicate constitutions can no longer take the obtrusive flash of cameras. Just yesterday, our esteemed president of the Seelie Court spent the afternoon in a daze, her nerves frazzled from the rays of one such human's photographing device. Lest the issue be solved shortly, we regretfully announce we shall no longer carry on with our commitments to the Order of Magickal Affairs, which has of course greatly benefited from our feats. In 1812, the venerable Tiny Treewart...

The letter had dragged on and on, listing the long history of diplomatic relationships between the Seelie Court and the Order of Magickal Affairs. It had been the first – and most polite – of a long series of letters of complaint, all revolving around a certain Axel Lacroix and his Haunted Crescent City Tour.

Ghosts, perturbed in their centuries-old routines because of the hordes of tourists that gathered behind the damned man to gawk at them. Werewolves, hunted down in their own woods on nights of full moon. Vampires, crying cultural appropriation as cheap human look alikes invaded the French Quarter... And Arla wasn't too keen on the way the man depicted witches as warty old hags either, she thought with a huff.

For centuries now, New Orleans had been a haven for supernatural beings of all shapes and sizes. And Arla's family could take much of the credit for that. The Alcaraz women had crafted a delicate balance between vampires and werewolves, that had lasted over two centuries. Only one measly human was turning them all into a freak show, exposing and ridiculing their deep-rooted magickal traditions. Arla's pride was so hurt, she clenched her fists to a painful degree.

I need to unwind, she told herself as she observed the crescent shaped marks her nails had dug into her skin. She scanned the room for a fun, relaxing activity to do. Given that she was at the morgue – one of Arla's favorite places on Earth – there were plenty of options to choose from.

Her eyes rested upon a pallid ghoul lying upon an autopsy table. Police were due to examine the corpse in a few hours, and there was no way Arla was letting humans see the beast in its current state. Grabbing a pair of sturdy nail clippers, she walked over to the miscreant she had been in charge of executing just last night.

Only the door flew open at that moment, and in came a curvy brunette with the wildest mop of auburn hair. Arla almost rolled her eyes at her younger sister's sprightly, disheveled appearance. She loved her dearly, but Zona was a true force of chaos. Everything she didn't need right now as her fingers continued to tense in fury.

"This is a federal institution you know," Arla pointed out in a clipped tone as she focused on the ghoul's ridiculously long claws. "You need more than just a pretty smile to enter."

Zona's bow-shaped lips formed into a smug smirk – and even then, she looked beautiful enough to send a pang of envy through Arla's heart. She mentally shook her head at herself. She was much too old to behave like a jealous ten year old.

"That cute little security guard you have parked out there

doesn't seem to think so," Zona drawled in that raspy, mellow voice of hers. "And give me a break. I'm your sister. I know what you do."

Arla muttered something about how it was a question of principles, and did her best to focus her foul mood on the ghoul's nails. Only her mind kept fleeting back to the O.M.A letter in her drawer, and the maddening face of the human she had yet to see. Word had it Axel Lacroix was quite the ladies' man. That just made Arla want to throttle him even more.

Heels resonated through the tiled room. Arla's heavy-duty nail clippers were flung out of her hands, as Zona took over the task.

"Whatever is bothering you, it's no excuse for what you're doing to this poor ghoul," her sister scolded gently. "Mom always taught us to show more respect for the dead than the living. You should know better."

Arla gasped in horror. Somehow in her blind bout of fury, she had managed to bend each of the ghoul's long, bony fingers backwards at the most unnatural angle. That would never pass human inspection.

"Thanks," Arla muttered as she sank into a chair. "I had my mind on something."

"Duh. Again, I'm your sister. I can tell when you're bugged because there's a fly on your knee." Zona looked at her pointedly. "There's a fly on your knee."

Arla jerked and batted the offending creature away, more than a little flustered by how uncannily perceptive her sister was. She gulped. *Does Zona know?* Did she know how green with envy Arla had always been, from the first time she laid eyes on a beautiful baby with the most stunning emerald gaze, until this very instant?

The two sisters couldn't have been more different. Arla had been a dark, scrawny child, and she hadn't grown much more pleasant to the eye. Zona, on the other hand, was like the sun to her darkness. Adults always sported a smile as they watched the little redhead frolic around, forever up to some kind of mischief.

Though only five years separated them, Arla came to the world with a lifetime's worth more responsibility. Not that she resented it – on the contrary, she thanked her lucky stars that she was born first. The title of Reaper was passed on from mother to daughter in the Alcaraz family, and it was a duty that only one could carry at a time.

As demanding a calling as it was, Arla loved her job. She loved the purpose it gave to her life. And she loved being good at it.

Most would think harvesting misbehaving souls would be an action-packed line of work, but the truth was Arla spent a lot of time behind a desk. Analyzing, negotiating, digging out old files… Those were things Arla excelled at. The O.M.A had applauded her finesse in laying down supernatural law in the New Orleans area more than once, and that was something that made Arla pretty damn proud.

She gazed at Zona, who trimmed the ghoul's nails with all the expertise of a beautician. In a way, Arla pitied her gorgeous sister. While she had been hit with all kinds of heavy responsibilities from a young age, Zona had always been left footloose and fancy free. Maybe a handful of times, Arla had wished their mother would let her traipse around in the fields too, instead of dragging her along on some morbid mission. But at the end of the day, Arla would rather feel burdened than have the kind of restless, aimless energy that seemed to torment Zona.

"Care to tell me what's on your mind," her sister asked in a light tone that sounded a little forced, "or is it too important to share with little old me?"

Though she kept her lovely traits calm and composed, her

lush green eyes were a shade darker than usual. Arla could tell there was irritation brewing in there.

"Well, I suppose it kind of involves you too, actually," Arla sighed wearily.

A spark of interest lit Zona's jade gaze. "Really?" She breathed a little too enthusiastically. "There's something I need to do?"

"Not really, no. I just mean that it's a case that touches upon our family name."

An awkward silence filled the room, only interrupted with the sound of the nail clippers.

"I don't have the title that most of the women in our family carry, but my last name is still Alcaraz, you know."

Arla's heart twinged. "It's classified information, Zo," she murmured gently.

A hardness replaced the excited glimmer that had animated Zona moments ago. "Right," she blurted coldly. "Sorry, I shouldn't pester you."

"It's Axel Lacroix again," Arla found herself explaining. She hated that hurt look on her little sister's face. "The idiot behind Haunted Crescent City Tours."

Recognition flashed across her fair features. "That hunky human who's been making a mess of the hearts of every witch, vampiress, she-wolf and ghostess in town?"

Arla scowled. "He's been causing a lot more trouble than a few broken hearts. Don't you remember the fairies? They keep going on strike now."

Zona shook her head as she looked for the nail file. "Those fairies are such wimps. Don't tell me they can't handle a few tourists."

"A few? Do you have any idea how much paranormal tourism has exploded since Lacroix started his silly little ghost tour?" Arla bolted up and waved towards the diagrams and charts scattered across her desk. "We're talking about creatures of the night, Zona. Beings that are meant to live in the shadows, not under the flash of cameras!"

"Someone's got her knickers in a twist."

Arla huffed and fell back onto her seat. "I can't stand the way he treats supernatural beings so callously. Last night he knocked out a Letiche!"

Her sister snorted. "Good. Those things are so ugly. And they stink."

"Zona!" Arla roared, outraged. "O.M.A classifies the Letiche as an endangered magickal species!"

Holding her hands up in apology, her sister sent her a sheepish smile. "Okay, okay. I'll be good." After a few seconds, she cocked her head with a slight frown. "But what was he doing all the way over in the swamps at night? That's an odd place for a human to be."

Arla bobbed her head up and down much too eagerly, aware of the wild strands of kinky black hair escaping from her braids. "Yes, it is, isn't it? And can't you think of something that's buried deep in the bayou, where no decent mortal should have any business at all?"

Zona's eyes went wide as saucers. A small part of Arla took pleasure as she finally witnessed the shock and fear spread over her sister's face.

"The Mori mirror?" Zona whispered in a broken voice. Upon Arla's grim silence, she stammered: "But… How could he…? He's just a regular human. How could he get past Great Grandma's spell?"

Arla nodded slowly, feeling oddly relieved after sharing some of her worries. "I know, right? It's so weird. O.M.A attributes it to an unusual flood that made the coffin rise above ground, but I'm pretty sure Philomena's magick is stronger than that."

She jumped as a sudden snap echoed through the room.

Her eyes zeroed in on the ghoul's mangled hand. It was missing a finger now. Zona must have broken it off.

Arla's heart broke as she watched her sister stand in the middle of the room, her traits twisted with pure terror. She hadn't anticipated such a reaction from her sister – even she hadn't been quite so affected by the news.

"It'll be alright, Zo," she murmured with as much confidence as she could muster. "I'll get this under control."

"But if the vampires or the werewolves find out…"

"It will be a catastrophe, yes," Arla finished grimly. "That's why I need to discreetly get this Axel Lacroix to tell me the whereabouts of the mirror, and then… " She made a crude gesture across her neck as if she were chopping it off. Oh, the joy when she would finally execute him however she saw fit.

"But how will you get him to spill the beans? A truth serum would take a whole moon cycle to brew, and we don't have that kind of time."

"I'm a little stumped on that one. O.M.A suggested using seduction, but I'm not sure I approve of that kind of method," she said stiffly.

Of course, the truth was she wasn't confident she could pull it off even if she tried. Arla liked to think herself a fairly capable witch, but plain old charm was a kind of magick that was beyond her.

"Bingo!" Zona cried, the color coming back to her cheeks. "For once those old fogies at the Order got it right!" She slung an arm around Arla's shoulders. "Listen, I'll do it for you, okay? Obviously driving a man crazy is more my area of expertise. Give me one night with him. Just one. And I'll get you the information."

Mirth danced across those green depths, but Arla felt her insides knotting with resentment.

"Then you can chop his head off, cut him up in pieces, or have fun doing whatever you usually like to do."

Arla's heart froze. All of a sudden the arm around her didn't feel like her sister's but like a vise, smothering her with feelings of inadequacy that she had never really managed to shake off. Why did it seem so obvious, even to her, that Zona was the only one fit to charm a man out of his wits?

She had checked herself in the mirror this morning. Sure, she was flat most of the places her sister was curvy. And unlike the reddish hue of Zona's hair and the green of her eyes, Arla's were just plain black. But she wasn't ugly. Not by far. She liked the way she could hold her gaze strong and steady, and her trim figure was something many women her age would envy. She was just a bit less... dazzling than her sister, perhaps.

Clearing her throat and shrugging out of Zona's hold, Arla looked everywhere but at her. "Thank you, but this is my job, Zona. I'll take care of it. Don't worry."

The redhead frowned and tried to peer into Arla's gaze, but she did a great job at dodging it. "Are you sure, Arla?"

Just when Arla was about to snap that she could take her concern for her and her lack of sex appeal and shove it, Zona's next words made her guts twist with guilt: "I just thought you would feel uncomfortable doing that kind of thing. But if you feel up to it... I know you'll do a great job. You always do."

Arla was still struggling to answer, when Zona picked up her purse and walked towards the door. "Anyhow, got to go. I'm meeting some friends tonight, and... Well good luck, okay?"

Arla barely had time to nod before she was gone.

The light was dwindling outside her window, yet Arla could still be found in her office, slaving through the pile of paperwork on her desk that never ceased to accumulate.

Exceptional gremlins intervention scheduled on the third night of the new moon. Humans shall be evacuated beforehand by means of magick. Regular service shall be assured by 7AM the following morning.

Arla peered through the curtains. That was tonight, right? Feeling strangely empty after the day's conversation, she certified her approval with a red star-shaped stamp and moved on to the next document. *Confirmation of the eradication of the misbehaving ghoul?* Stamp.

Axel Lacroix. Mandate for immediate execution.

Arla went through the contents of the letter again, this time with her sister's words echoing through her mind. *Obviously driving a man crazy is more my area of expertise.*

And Zona was right. How many years had she and Samuel been together, and she had never heard him so much as utter the L word? She added the numbers up, and then her heart dropped – nineteen years. Nineteen years since they had been involved with each other on and off, and she had hardly ever seen more than a twinkle in the man's grey eyes.

Who are you kidding, she admonished herself. *How in the world are you going to do with Axel Lacroix in one night what you never managed to do with Samuel in nineteen years?*

And then it came to her. *How in the world, huh? Well, with magick of course,* a pesky little voice murmured in her head.

Arla groaned and hid her face in her hands. How pathetic was that – to rely on spells and illusions to fool a man into seduction. But there was no other way. She couldn't. She simply couldn't seduce the information out of Alex Lacroix's lips without a little help. And she couldn't lose face to her sister either.

Feeling sneaky, Arla rose from her swiveling chair and drew the curtains. Then she crouched down and rummaged through her boxes, until she laid hands on thirteen little red candles. Disposing them in a circle, she lit them one by one and said the incantation while using her hands to shape the magick in the air into doing her bidding. To most people, it might simply look like she was using a strange kind of sign language, but the adept and other magickal creatures could see the spell being woven.

The second Axel Lacroix would clap eyes upon her, she would become the most irresistible woman in the world for thirteen hours. With each hour, a candle would die, taking away with it some of the magick.

And when the charm wore off, no-one, not even Zona, would ever know about her little secret. Axel Lacroix would be dead. The Mori mirror would be hers again, and the two hundred year old peace the Alcaraz witches had fought to maintain could carry on as before.

AXEL

hat wasted old crook, Axel grumbled to himself as he shoved open the doors of the Last Barrel Bar. *Friends?* He snorted. *The two of you can drown in an ocean of rum together, he'll always be a pirate through and through.*

Drowning.... A wave of nausea rolled in his stomach at the memory of last night. His arm jerked of its own accord, as if he were still out there on the bayou, struggling with some god-awful slimy, stinky monster. For the hundredth time at least since he had made it back to New Orleans, Axel buried his nose in the crook of his elbow. No matter how much he scrubbed and lathered it with soap, he still detected the faint stench of the swamps on his skin. Or maybe it was just his imagination. All the same, Axel fought the urge to gag in the middle of the crowded bar.

And all that for what...? Axel shoved his way past the drunk tourists, ready to dump all his foul mood upon the pirate ghost.

"So what was the woman supposed to look at?" He snapped the moment he reached the dark corner the phantom in a tricorne hat always haunted. Fumbling inside his jacket, Axel dropped the offending object on the table. "Air?"

The clatter of silver on wood was drowned out by the loud partygoers everywhere around. Pierre St. Patin looked down, and a flash of recognition crossed his usually blank eyes. There, on the tabletop, sat the cause of Axel's frustration.

The silver handle gleamed like moonshine, even after two centuries under the ground. It was exquisitely adorned with crescent shaped crystals, so clear and brilliant they almost seemed to radiate light beams of their own. Axel was no connoisseur, but he knew these gems weren't the junk imitations they sold in the French Quarter for tourists. The oval frame was delicate and ornate as well, with a string of mysterious shapes and engravings.

All in all, Pierre St. Patin may not have been so far off when he had said it was worth all the sugar in the Caribbeans. Except one thing was missing.

"Where the hell is the mirror?" Axel barked, all his exhaustion and disappointment surging as the pirate didn't react. "Damn it, is it even a mirror if there's nothing to look into?"

Except now the hint of alertness in the weary ghost was gone. His gaze was empty as ever, as he peered into times Axel couldn't see, days he could never go back to.

"I had me a little cabin out there in the woods. Nothin' grand. But my Adelaide, she loved it."

Axel rolled his eyes. "Spare me. I created the first ghost tour business in New Orleans, remember? I know everything about the cabin you haunt back in the bayou." Exhausted, he slumped on his chair and gestured to the barman to bring him a glass of rum. "I even have a calendar of each documented ghost haunting in the region. So cut the crap. Was the mirror –"

"Back home, my wife Ciboulette, she would always be naggin' 'bout the rum. Would be clutchin' her Good Book, and yellin' me words 'bout if a man steals an ox or a sheep. Hell, damnation and all that. I tell her I'm no bilge-sucking livestock thief. This old pirate wants gold! And –"

"Pierre," Axel interrupted, in no mood for the ghost's rambles. Somehow, his old friend seemed even more scatter-brained than usual tonight. "The mirror. Was it like this when you buried it with Adelaide?"

Pierre St. Patin's eyes sparkled when he heard his beloved's name. "But in our cabin, Adelaide wouldn't bug me with none of that. Nay, she'd cook me a feast of creamed possum in coon fat gravy. And then we'd make sweet, tender love. We –"

"But when she died," Axel cut in. "The mirror. Was it –"

"Mind you, our bellies needn't be filled with creamed possum to play Nug-A-Nug. Nay, the sheets be shakin' before too!"

Axel knew when to recognize a lost cause. So he took a big swig from the drink the waiter handed him, and let the pirate rattle on about the same old stories, interjecting the occasional "ooh" or "aah". Nobody seemed to find it strange that Axel talked alone. After all, his behavior was perhaps the least bizarre in a bar full of tipsy tourists. At the other end of the room, one man was making a show of pretending to be a werewolf stuck mid-shift. He had gathered quite a crowd.

Axel shook his head. The lunar phase for wolves had passed, and tonight was a moonless night. But then, most humans believed things like vampires, witches and were-wolves were just the stuff of myths. Most humans liked the thrill of a good ghost story. Yet when morning came, they dusted off their pants, polished their shoes, and marched off to whatever respectable job they had. Monsters of the night and all that nonsense were forgotten.

Axel wasn't that kind of human.

Day and night, he dealt with supernaturals. Striking deals with them, tricking them, trapping them… Monsters were his business – and it was a very lucrative one. Unlike his ghost tour rivals who gathered secondhand accounts, Axel always worked on the field.

And from his decades scouring every old, creaking house and dark alley in New Orleans, Axel had noticed something interesting: supernaturals in the crescent city were obsessed with a certain mirror. Respectable vampires and werewolves were remarkably tight-lipped about the subject, and rogue supernaturals like St. Patin were too lunatic to give him much information. But one thing was sure: whatever magick this mirror wielded, it drew creatures from all over the world.

It can't be because they're vain, Axel thought grimly as he gazed at the mirrorless frame. Most supernaturals were just about as ugly as they could be, in his opinion. Ears that looked like bat wings, extra eyeballs or a surplus of bodily hair… He shivered.

No, beings of the night were nasty, power hungry things. The mirror must give some kind of incredible strength, some kind of supremacy over all other creatures… and that was exactly what Axel wanted. He wanted to dominate monsters once and for all, to have them scrabbling under his heel.

"I got me mind to go back to the cabin. See if the lass is there. She liked to pull 'em weeds out of the garden, and she would hum the sweetest tune. Lemme see if I can remember how it goes."

To Axel's horror, the demented pirate began to sing in a voice ravaged by too many cigars and several centuries worth of drinking:

"Hail, oh hail, ye happy spirits –"

"Yeah, well your haunting at the cabin isn't scheduled

until next month," Axel said hastily, covering his ears to the ear-splitting chant.

"But my Adelaide could be there now," Pierre St. Patin muttered with an eternity of sadness washing over his weathered face. "For all ye know, she's... Stuck, like me. Welcomed nor by life, nor by death."

Axel gulped as the last shreds of frustration from the night before were swept away. Over the decades he had known Pierre, the ghost had only gone from bad to worse. Of course the rum hadn't helped, but who could blame the old man for drinking himself into oblivion? His existence was an endless cycle, that revolved around one thing that he could never get back – a girl who was nothing but a pile of bones now.

Axel almost puked as he was hit with the memory of last night. A decaying coffin. A rotting skeleton. Delicate hands, folded over a beautiful but empty mirror. An unfamiliar feeling surged through him, that made his throat tight and his face prickle. Something that felt a bit like shame.

He bolted up and trudged towards the door. Halfway out the bar, he realized he had forgotten the mirror. But looking back, there were just too many people. That, and the old pirate ranting at the same table he had sat at for two centuries, next to a broken memento of his long-lost love was one of the saddest things Axel had ever seen.

Oh well, he sighed, *it's not like it'll be of any use to me.*

Axel set off through the French Quarter. *Damn it, I don't have anymore tricks up my sleeve. Got to come up with something else to keep the business going, or those rats at Witching Hour Tours will eat me up alive.* With a sneer, he ripped a few of his rival's posters off a wall, and continued to wander through the dark streets.

After his smelly adventures in the swamp last night, and the lousy evening tonight was turning out to be, Axel figured he really needed to unwind. Maybe he could pay a visit to Morgana, the sensual voodoo queen who had confectioned the gris-gris that enabled him to see ghosts – a 7 ingredient pouch made just for him, containing African ginger, crow feathers and a strand of hair from the clairvoyant herself. He had stuffed a few condoms in his back pocket right before leaving his house, eager for a wild night that would wash some of his weariness away.

"Hey Hippolyte," he called when he noticed a familiar silhouette slumped against a lamppost. "Don't forget to brush your teeth for tomorrow's tour. Got it?"

The gaunt vampire swirled around and snarled at him, flashing the most bloodshot pair of eyes in the whole haunted city of New Orleans.

"Give me a raise, or I may have one of your pretty little humans for dinner one of these days."

Axel shook his head as he made his way towards the haggard creature. The rogue vampire was a favorite with tourists. Axel couldn't have him sucking the blood out of them.

"Now now, Hippolyte. You know that's not how we work at Haunted Crescent City Tours." Handing him a bottle of possum blood Axel had concocted from the animals in his garden, he plastered on a smile. "Here, take some of this, okay? Consider it a bonus for posing with the kids last week. They loved you."

Hippolyte snatched the bottle and chugged it down. The bloodsucker was in hot water with the Clan, and had been left to survive by his own means – which, for a vampire, meant withering away in the streets, as feeding from humans was a capital crime in the supernatural world. If not for Axel, Hippolyte would have either lost his mind to starvation, either been executed for preying upon humans.

"Keep the fangs clean, okay? See you at seven on the dot tomorrow."

With that Axel continued to meander through the Vieux Carré. *How can I make them all as pathetic as Hippolyte?* Most of the city's renegade supernaturals were under his thumb, but vampires from the Clan of Nox and wolves from the Garou Pack still ruled the nights. The mirror was moot, so…

All of a sudden a strange prickling sensation crept up the back of his neck. He came to a halt. Axel was no clairvoyant, but years of hunting down monsters had fine-tuned his sixth sense – and whatever it was, something was off in this dark, misty part of town.

Allons, don't slow down boy, Grandma Tabby would always urge on their way home, *you know M'su Diable likes to linger at crossroads.* Axel's head shot towards each direction of the intersection. But the night was too dark and murky to see anything.

Cursing himself for straying from the crowded streets of the Quarter, Axel grabbed the dagger he always carried and sped up his pace.

Wait… Is that a woman over there? Out of the corner of his eye, he thought he spotted a stiff, yet distinctly feminine figure. A moment after, only fog swirled where the silhouette had been.

None too eager to prove his intuition true, Axel dashed in the opposite direction. He could hear faint noises from Bourbon Street. The music, the laughter, the catcalls. He needed to get where there were people. Fast.

Then he saw it. At the turn of the street, a rope of black hair drifted by in the distance. Axel shifted right, taking a small paved passage. But sure enough, at the far end of the alley, he saw something that made his blood chill.

Of all the women I have wronged, Axel thought in a panic,

was I really so bad that one of them would have a personal vendetta against me?

Actually, he could think of a few. Most recently a two hundred year old slave girl whose coffin he had unnailed.

Somehow though, he doubted that if Adelaide chose to come back, she would go for a pair of very modern looking black boots. He gulped. Waiting for him at the end of the lonely street, was the silhouette of a long leather-clad leg, with heels so pointy they could impale a man.

His heart pounded so hard it almost bursted out of his chest. Without a second to spare, Axel launched into a wild sprint through the French Quarter. He never took the time to look back. The echo of footsteps followed him, until they didn't anymore. Or maybe they were drowned down by the happy brouhaha of tipsy tourists and jazz clubs.

You made it, Axel told himself as he wound down on the bustling Bourbon Street. *You escaped the she-devil that was out for your hide.* Laughter bubbled in his chest. He almost could have accompanied the relief that washed through him with a swig of daiquiri.

But when his mirth died down, his ears were still ringing hollowly. His entire body felt light and shaky, as if he had only narrowly dodged disaster. As if at the very last moment he had taken a turn, because whatever was waiting for him at the end of the road would change his fate forever. Axel had no rational explanation, but his sixth sense told him that nothing would have ever looked the same anymore, had he walked down that alley.

And I'm pretty doggone happy with my life just the way it is, Axel thought ruefully. There was just the problem of all these copycat tours cropping up in New Orleans, and the fact that the Clan of Nox and the Garou Pack were still powerful as ever. But those were things Axel could change with time. He loved the kind of money he made, he loved the women he got, he loved the helpless look he put in the eyes of Hippolyte and the like. Whatever fate had awaited him in tall leather boots, Axel did not want.

As Axel caught his breath, hordes of rowdy partygoers pushed forward. He stood straight and followed the flow. He was safe now. No self-respecting supernatural would attack him in such a crowd. Blatant displays of magic were strictly prohibited.

Dozens of people brushed past him, but all of a sudden his skin tingled with eerie awareness again. It was but for a fraction of a second, yet his whole body sprang back to alertness when cool, smooth skin grazed his arm.

She's here, he realized with a chill. *She's behind me, I can feel it.* Suddenly Bourbon Street and its happy cacophony died down. Of the hundreds of voices around him, all he could hear was the god-awful sound of those spiked heels hitting the pavement. And all he could think was, *don't look back.* Axel felt it in his gut. If he cared at all for his life – and he did, big-time – he must not look back.

"Hey, you. Your shoelace is undone, you know?"

Huh. Really?

Sure enough, it was. And then stupidly, thoughtlessly, Axel peered behind.

Eyes black and hard as onyx stared back at him. Wide and bold, they were slightly buggy on an otherwise lean face. The strict line of her nose was broken by a small bump, giving her a bit of a hawkish air. Her lips weren't exactly thin, but they were a far cry from the full, lush ones Axel usually went for.

For someone so ominous she made his blood run cold, the woman was surprisingly short. There wasn't much softness to her, as her arms were slim but strong, and her narrow hips led to lithe legs clad in those tall, spine-chilling black boots.

"You should tie your shoelace, handsome. I don't want you falling for someone else."

An odd sensation hit Axel. As if he was standing at the moment before all hell broke loose. As if there was a crack in the dam.

One second, the stranger's words were just about the worst pick-up line he had ever heard. And the pair of black eyes scrutinizing him was the most sinister he had ever seen.

Then Axel was knocked by a huge, irresistible force. Everything around him blacked out. First it felt like a thick fog entered his mind. It was pleasant, frightfully so. *This has got to be magick*, the little voice in his head moaned before it withered away.

But all of a sudden it was like his brain was being compressed, crammed into a funnel. Pain exploded in either side of his head. The inkling that maybe he was going to die didn't cross his mind – he couldn't think that far anymore. But all the same, his heart hammered with terror.

Then the agony stopped. It was like the storm blazing in his mind suddenly came to an end, leaving place to a flat, tranquil sea. He could see again.

So the next second, when he looked up, his eyes were met with something wonderful. There, right before him, stood the most bewitching woman in the world!

GRAB IT NOW!

Psychic's Temptation

Mermaid's Call

Warlock's Claim

Historical Paranormal Romance

Secrets of Storyville

A Countess Betrayed

A Harlot Betrothed

Epic World Building Academy Romance

The Broken Academy

Power of Fire

Power of Magic

Power of Blood

Pacts & Promises

Bonds

Reverse Harem Escapes – Great for a Quick Roll in the Hay with None of the Guilt

Fated Shifter Mates

Mated to the Pack

Mated to Team Shadow

Mated to the Pride

Taming Her Bears

Mated to the Clan

Protected by the Pack

Claimed by the Pack

The Descendants :

Desired by Four

Fate of Three

Shared by the Four

Mates & Magic

The Sharing Spell

The Spell's Price

Backfired Magic